SLOCUM WAS PLUMB TUCKERED OUT FROM KEEPING UP WITH TWO JOBS AT ONCE.

The first was what he had been hired to do: handle cattle on the sprawling, swampy land that was the Calder ranch. But these tropical cowboys had a different way of doing everything. There wasn't a hand among them who could be sure of hitting the ground with a rope if he dropped it. But any one of them could make a bullwhip stand up and talk.

The other job was trying to keep up with the insatiable and still growing demands of Rose Calder.

Not that Slocum minded exactly. But a man has to sleep sometime....

OTHER BOOKS BY JAKE LOGAN

RIDE, SLOCUM, RIDE
HANGING JUSTICE
SLOCUM AND THE WIDOW KATE
ACROSS THE RIO GRANDE
THE COMANCHE'S WOMAN
SLOCUM'S GOLD
BLOODY TRAIL TO TEXAS
NORTH TO DAKOTA
SLOCUM'S WOMAN
WHITE HELL
RIDE FOR REVENGE
OUTLAW BLOOD
MONTANA SHOWDOWN
SEE TEXAS AND DIE
IRON MUSTANG
SHOTGUNS FROM HELL
SLOCUM'S BLOOD
SLOCUM'S FIRE
SLOCUM'S REVENGE
SLOCUM'S HELL
SLOCUM'S GRAVE
DEAD MAN'S HAND
FIGHTING VENGEANCE
SLOCUM'S SLAUGHTER
ROUGHRIDER
SLOCUM'S RAGE
HELLFIRE
SLOCUM'S CODE
SLOCUM'S FLAG
SLOCUM'S RAID
SLOCUM'S RUN
BLAZING GUNS
SLOCUM'S GAMBLE
SLOCUM'S DEBT
SLOCUM AND THE MAD MAJOR
THE NECKTIE PARTY
THE CANYON BUNCH

JAKE LOGAN

SWAMP FOXES

PLAYBOY
PAPERBACKS

1

Slocum came awake instantly, with no period of transition between sleep and wakefulness. His eyes opened but he lay completely still as he listened, making sure that it was not some unremembered hint of noise that had brought him awake. There was nothing that seemed out of place, and after a moment he let himself relax.

Despite that caution born of long habit and a desire to preserve his own life for as long a period as possible, John Slocum was momentarily disoriented. That was to be expected, perhaps. He seldom had an opportunity to sleep in one bed twice, and a permanent home was something he no longer gave thought to.

This place now . . . he looked around the small, rented room in the first gray light of the predawn. It would be a hotel. Had to be. It was like a thousand others he had flopped in, from Canada to Mexico and back again. Small of size, bare of walls, the furnishings kept to a rough-and-ready minimum, and all constructed cheaply and sturdily so that it would take more than your average drunk to do any real damage. That much was all right.

Slocum's nostrils flared in his lean, darkly handsome face, and he remembered where he was. The quality of the air and the various scents it carried told him that much.

The room was hot, and the air was damply humid. There was no blanket on the bed, and the single sheet that was pulled up to chin level stuck moistly to his naked body. So he was down along the coast. Anywhere inland would have been much drier.

The heavy, fetid odor of rotting meat pinned it down even more. Packing houses. More than one of them.

He remembered now. Rockport, down on the Texas coastline. He was on his way to Brownsville where he was to meet Harry Martin and a man named Valdez. It sounded like it would be a sweetheart deal all the way around.

Harry had reached him by way of a mutual acquaintance, a bartender in Cheyenne. The way Slocum understood it, Harry had access to a nearly limitless supply of rifles and ammunition. Probably, Slocum guessed, surplus junk from the War for Southern Independence. All breach loaders, which meant that they were probably conversions to that bastard offspring .58-70 caliber that temporarily bridged the gap between the .58-caliber front loaders and the .50-70 that the Springfield Armory turned out for the Army.

Not that Slocum cared. They could have been rusty Gallaghers for all he cared.

The point was that they were in demand now below the border, and Harry had a source for them.

Valdez was supposed to have a supply of gold coins that was about as limitless as Harry Martin's supply of rifles. That struck Slocum as being a fine-and-dandy match-up.

John Slocum came into it because Harry Martin had a fine talent for selling guns but no ability at all when it came to using them. As for Valdez, Slocum did not know. Nor care. Harry needed someone to handle a delivery system that would give the least likelihood of losing the merchandise to the wrong side; i.e., to someone who was not paying for them. To Harry, the right side would be the one with the cash, and in this deal that seemed to be Valdez. Obviously Harry was not willing to trust his other-side-of-the-border partner to take care of security and delivery, so he had called in Slocum with a promise of 15 percent of the take. A sweetheart deal if Slocum had ever heard one. Good old

Harry. Slocum loved him like a brother. At least until this deal was done.

Which explained Rockport. It was between Cheyenne and Brownsville.

And an overnight stop was about all John Slocum could stand of Rockport, Texas.

Helluva place. Weary and fading fast was the way he read it. From the number of buildings along the wharf area, which was just about all of Rockport, this must have been some kind of booming place a few years earlier, but now most of the packinghouses were dead or dying; they were either empty already or soon would be.

During the war and just afterward, he vaguely remembered hearing someone say, the place had been a-boom with the shipment of beef hides and tallow. That was all beef was good for in those days; because there were no railheads to ship cattle to market, there was no way to preserve the meat once the beeves were slaughtered. When the Kansas railheads were opened, though, it was a death blow for the town. The locals couldn't afford to pay slaughterhouse prices just to get the hides and tallow, and so the town was slowly dying.

Served it right, Slocum thought as he pulled a patch of damp sheet away from his skin and shoved it away from him.

He yawned and stretched and scratched his chest. It was like scratching warm marble. Slocum was about as fit as he had ever been in his life. Which was a damn good thing. It took a man in good condition to survive a drunk like the one John Slocum had put on the night before. As it was, his head was cracked a little but not splitting open, and except for the vile taste in his mouth he felt downright decent. He stretched again and hoped he had had as good a time as he thought he must have.

The bed was lumpy, and Slocum moved aside to try to fit himself into a few valleys between the hillocks of the mattress.

He found an exceptionally large lump and began to

grin, because this lump was longer than most and seemed to have a long spill of shining black hair spreading out of the upper end of it.

Fancy that, Slocum thought. He stripped the sheet off his bed partner and the grin got wider.

The girl was dressed exactly the same way Slocum was, and he was wearing nothing at all.

Since she was lying down he couldn't tell how tall she was, but who cared. Her face, relaxed and innocent— he hoped that part was a dirty lie—in sleep, was pretty if a trifle short of ravingly beautiful. Full lips. Finely molded nose. Gracefully arched brows. Long, curling lashes that lay now dark and lovely against the pale, smooth skin of her cheeks. Her chin was a bit small, which was the only thing that kept her out of that "raving" category.

But if her chin was undersized, the same could not be said about her breasts. Everything her chin lacked her chest made up for, and then some. Globular and as full as ripe melons, *they* were something to rave over. They jutted firm and proud from a slender frame that nipped in to a remarkably narrow waist and swelled again to a wide, rounded mound of hip and rump. Below that was a long, shapely flow of leg. Legs, actually. There were two of them. Slocum counted. Then he counted her breasts again. Two of those, too. Just to make sure the girl wasn't trying to fool him about that, he thought he'd better handle them some. An expert can do amazing things with mirrors, and Slocum wanted to be sure.

He reached out and ran his palm first over one rose-tipped nipple and then the other. He had been right. Two of those, also. And certainly more than a mouthful there for a man to play with.

My oh my, Slocum thought to himself. Whoever made up that old saying about more than a mouthful being wasted was purely full of shit, Slocum thought. An abundance like this was anything but a waste.

There was more than a handful there, too. He tried it

out just to make sure. He was right again, by damn. Definitely more than a handful.

His kneading and pawing penetrated the girl's sleep, which was exactly what Slocum intended. If his chest was like marble, that was nothing but mush in comparison with the tent pole that was poking up toward the ceiling now, bouncing and talking to him and telling him to do something about it before lack of use froze it in that condition and he had to go out and buy new and larger jeans just to accommodate the damned, demanding thing.

The girl stirred and opened her eyes blankly. She looked at him without comprehension at first, then said something to him in Spanish. Slocum shrugged, not comprehending.

She blinked and tried it again, this time in English. "Hallo, lover bay-bee."

Slocum winced. Maybe she should have kept it in Spanish. On the other hand . . . He looked at the Grand Tetons sprouting from her chest and reconsidered. The originals could not hold a candle to these mountains.

Hell, he thought, a lady doesn't have to be a conversationalist to be attractive.

She started to say something to him, but he had figured that one out already. After all, nobody can talk with their mouth full. He took a handful of glossy hair and gave her a little tug, sort of down and toward the side.

The girl's eyes cut sideways toward Slocum's face, but her view had to cross another point of major interest before it could reach its intended target. She saw and she understood. Her brown eyes widened, and a broad grin spread across her face. "Ooo, bay-bee." She clapped her hands lightly and giggled her pleasure. "For me?"

"*Sí*, sweetie," Slocum assured her. "Just for you." He sighed. He had no recollection at all what her name might be, and it hardly seemed an appropriate time to ask for an introduction. "Just for you."

She ran her fingertips over his balls and draped herself happily across Slocum's lower belly. She followed the fingertips with a flutter of pink tongue, and Slocum came very close to disappointing the both of them with a too-soon gush of superhot, sticky fluid. He managed to control himself just in time.

Slocum sighed and lay back on the slender excuse for a pillow the hotel had provided. He laced his hands behind his head and closed his eyes in contentment.

It felt like he was being engulfed in warmth and wetness as she worked up one side and down the other and finally down the middle.

It was for sure that this kid lacked a gag reflex, Slocum thought without a hint of displeasure at the omission.

He would have been willing for her to spend the newly dawning day just that way, but eventually she got tired of that form of play—or maybe her jaws just began to give out—and released him.

She squirmed around into a position on top of Slocum's chest, and for a moment he wondered what she was up to since she crossed her hands under his chin, winked at him and grinned.

"What . . . ?"

Then he knew. Damn!

The girl gave a little wiggle with her hips, and her grin got all the wider. Slocum felt himself slide deep and deeper into a wet and ready niche she had prepared just for him.

Damnation. And she hadn't hardly moved. She wiggled just that little bit and then there he was, deep inside where it was the warmest and the best. Now what? he wondered.

He didn't have to wait long for his answer.

The girl's hips never moved. There was not the least bit of rise and fall of her butt—he reached around and clamped his powerful hands around those firm cheeks just to make sure he was really feeling what he thought he was feeling—but he could feel a series of contractions *inside* the girl that was milking him with a slow, powerful pull. Damn, that felt good.

"Naw," he said. "You can't be . . ."

She laughed, a bright peal of delight, and nodded that she could indeed be. And was. She did it some more.

"Sonuvabitch," Slocum whispered thoughtfully. He took his big hands off the dimpled cheeks of her ass and applauded. Talent should be rewarded and encouraged wherever it is found.

"Gracias," she said happily.

She seemed to tire after a while, so Slocum did the gentlemanly thing. He rolled her over and took upon himself the burden of the labor.

Actually, he plowed into her hot and heavy as a kid tearing off his very first piece. That little Mexican girl had been able to get him some kind of worked up.

And when that frenzied burst of activity was used up, he slowed down and did it all over again with more dignity, as befits a grown man.

This was not, Slocum decided, a half-bad way to wake up of a morning.

2

Slocum was beginning to wonder if he *really* had to get south in such a huge hurry, or if maybe he should stay here and rest up for a day or three, when the decision was made for him.

One moment it was all peace and lassitude, with the warm, smooth haunch of the pretty little girl pressed up against the side of his hip.

The next there was hell to pay.

The flimsy slide-bolt lock on the cheap rented room burst forward like it had been shot from the barrel of a gun, and the door itself crashed open immediately behind it.

There were three of them. And at least two of them had knives in their hands.

Slocum required no time at all to assess those facts. He might have been feeling lazy on this particular morning, but he was a long way from dead, and his instincts took over. He was no longer looking at the men who had burst through the rudely opened doorway. Instead he was examining the details about them from a retinal image in his memory. Already, without thought, he was throwing himself aside and rolling for the bed-post where he had hung his gun belt the night before. Some things, like beds and bed partners, might change, but the placement of John Slocum's revolver ready and close to hand was one of life's constants.

That his visitors' intentions were serious, Slocum had no doubts. The one brief glance he had given them told him that all three were gentlemen of Mexican ancestry. And this was a Mexican girl he had so recently been enjoying. He did not think that the similarity was coincidental, and he damn sure didn't intend to wait for introductions or explanations. Experience indicated that he should be doing something, and damned fast.

The problem was that while John Slocum's intentions were every bit as obvious as those of the men who had already spilled through the doorway into the room, the results he was gaining from his efforts were somewhat less than he might have hoped.

In fact, he seemed to have a fourth adversary now. A rather pretty one. And she was crawling his frame like stink on shit.

Worse, the little bitch was keeping him from getting his hands on his holstered Colt.

She seemed to be shouting something about "no, don't, no, no" on the one hand and on the other was shouting something in Spanish that damn sure had a ring of "rape, rape" to it. Slocum was not particularly interested in getting a translation. He just wanted the hell out of there before her papa or brother or uncle or boyfriend or some combination thereof made an unpleasant connection between the blade of a knife and the ribs of one John Slocum.

"*Shit!*" Slocum roared.

He reached again for his gun, and the treacherous little bitch bit his hand. It hurt. Slocum clipped her in the jaw with his free hand to knock her teeth loose from his flesh.

It worked, but by that time the unhappy threesome of friends, relatives, or what-have-you had reached the damned bedside and snatched Slocum's own revolver from the post.

Enough was just about enough, Slocum thought. He rolled off the bed in the other direction in time to avoid a nasty slash from one of the knives.

By now the girl was bawling and pointing and making noises that sure sounded like accusations, and the three Mexicans—Slocum noticed that they looked like a basically clean-cut and respectable crowd and not your average bad-ass *bandidos*—were getting all the madder.

Slocum was on his feet now, facing them from across the rumpled and sweat-stained bedding. The three men were glaring at him. The girl was still yammering at the top of her well-constructed lungs.

"What the hell are you mad at me for?" Slocum demanded. "Look at 'er." He pointed. "Don't blame me. Hell, a sight like that'd make the Pope drop his drawers. Or whatever it is he wears under that fancy dress."

Pointing might have been a mistake. The men did look. And got all the madder.

One of them screamed something at him in rapid-fire Spanish. Another began tugging at the grips of Slocum's revolver, fortunately not noticing the raw-hide holster thong that kept the gun from sliding free.

The third man seemed more interested in direct and immediate action. He was coming around the end of the bed. And the knife he was carrying, held low and balanced like he knew what to do with it, was one mean-looking sonuvabitch of a weapon.

"I don't suppose you'd want to stop an' talk this over," Slocum said. "No," he answered himself. "I reckon maybe you wouldn't, at that."

Slocum adopted a casual pose, leaning on the back of a chair where he had flung his trousers the night before and giving the nearest knifeman a friendly grin. "Think it over."

The Mexican kept coming, crouched now and moving in slowly. The other two had quit paying attention to the girl and were backing him up.

Slocum grinned at them again. "Wish I could stay an' chat, but I got a business meeting to keep."

He grabbed his trousers off the chair and whirled. There was only one way out that he could see, and that was the window directly behind him. The three Mexicans were between him and the door, and he had less than no desire to run a gauntlet to reach it.

He launched himself in a dive through the window.

On his way out it occurred to him to wonder if this was a ground-floor room. Or maybe not.

3

Slocum sailed out the window in a shower of glass and splintered wood, hit the ground, and rolled. He came onto his feet with his pants still clutched in his left hand and began at once to hop out of the line of sight from the window, trying to move and to pull his trousers on at the same time. It was a situation more suitable to ribald jokes than to real life, and under other circumstances Slocum himself might have laughed. As it was, those men behind him were carrying real knives, and at least one of them held a real gun—Slocum's own—and he *knew* how good a weapon that was.

At least the damned rented room had been on the ground floor. He had no way of knowing whether his faith in that fact had been subliminal memory or blind luck. And he was not going to take time now to try to decide either way. Right now he just wanted the hell out of the way.

Slocum got his trousers waist-high and reached the side of the building at approximately the same time. Already, though, he could hear renewed shouting from the window he had just left, and he could see the foot of one man and the gun-wielding fist of another protruding beyond the shattered window frame.

Time to say adios, Slocum told himself.

Since he was already on that side of the building, he bolted down the street to his right. He could have ducked into an alley instead, but bare feet and broken bottles make poor companions. Slocum figured he had troubles enough without adding an injury to slow him down.

This was a helluva position to find himself in, espe-

17

cially a man with John Slocum's vast experience, he reflected as he ran. Unarmed and all but undressed, with a screaming woman and a bunch of irate kin behind him. Shee-it!

This also was not the time to think about it. He ran.

Slocum's bare feet pounded down the dirt street, becoming quite thoroughly bruised on the sharp bits of shell and gravel underfoot. He did not take the time that would have been necessary to worry about that.

Behind him he could hear even more shouts. Either the men were gaining on him or they had picked up some friends along the way.

He glanced over his shoulder. There were just the three of them, but they were definitely closer than he wanted to see them.

The one—thank goodness there was only one—with the revolver raised the weapon—Slocum's weapon—and snapped off a quick, unaimed shot.

There was little danger that one running man could hit another, particularly someone who was not expert with firearms, but there was always the danger of dumb luck entering the picture. The bullet sizzled uncomfortably close to Slocum's ear, and he redoubled his efforts.

The street ahead was short. Hell, there wasn't enough to the town of Rockport to give it any street more than a few blocks long. And there seemed to be no place at all around there to hide.

It was ignominious as hell, Slocum realized. A man of his stature having to hide from a bunch of whooped-up yahoos with knives and a mad-on about his hard-on. But the only alternative would seem to be a knife blade in the gut, and that Slocum could do without. He ran blindly on. Those bastards behind them were quicker on their feet than John Slocum wanted them to be.

The street ended abruptly, and the dirt and shell surface underfoot turned to wooden planking. Slocum kept running.

He was on a wharf or a dock now, he could see. Given a choice, he would have darted off to the side;

but dammit, he was out onto the planks before he realized what they were.

And those damned Mexicans were practically at his heels. As if to remind him of that fact, the one with the gun tried another couple snap shots in Slocum's direction. He had no idea where those bullets went, but the noise was enough to lend additional speed to his pumping legs.

Although just where it was that he was going, well, that remained to be seen. There just was not a whole hell of a lot of wharf left in front of him.

Slocum put his head down and raced ahead of his pursuers. He was in excellent physical condition—a man in Slocum's position had to be—and he was beginning to get his second wind now, beginning to pay more attention to what lay ahead as well as to what lay immediately behind.

Ahead there was, most definitely, the end of the damned wharf.

Fair enough, Slocum thought. He could swim, and with those knife-toting idiots behind him he was just betting that he could swim like a sonuvabitch. Probably fast enough to throw a wake that would rock ships at the other end of the harbor. He prepared himself for a fast dive into whatever slop lay below the end of the wharf.

Slocum put his head down and his arms up and was already in the process of launching himself into the air when he saw that he had fucked up again.

There was no damned water down there. Not right beneath him, there wasn't.

Instead there was a long, wide boat, the kind they called a lighter, bobbing in the trash-filled water at the end of the dock. Slocum had time to see that the boat was occupied and that a number of oddly dressed men were at the oars. That was all the time he had to ponder his new discovery.

With his last, tenuous touch of toe to planking, John Slocum kicked out with all the power he could muster.

If he was not able to extend his dive all the way over the damned lighter he was going to go face-first into the gunwales and end up without a tooth in his head. Assuming that he would still have a usable head left.

Shee-it!

He jumped and gave it all he had.

4

Slocum's leg hurt like some damned Kiowa had jammed a spear point into it. He had cleared the far gunwale of the boat . . . almost. His right thigh had clipped the edge, and now he could feel a cramp coming on. The pain was momentary, he knew, but still it was intense enough to make swimming, or even treading water, very nearly impossible. Given a choice between dying with a knife in his guts and drowning, Slocum would, on the whole, prefer to still be asleep in his bed.

"Give you a hand, mate?"

Slocum's head jerked up, and a spray of water droplets flew through the humid air. The side of the lighter was looming directly above him, and a beard-stubbled face was peering over the side. "Huh?"

"I asked d'ya want a hand."

"Reckon I could use one," Slocum agreed drily. Which was difficult under the circumstances.

The head Slocum could see was joined by a pair of others. The men leaned over to reveal powerful sets of arms with ropes of muscle cording them and equally brawny shoulders. Among them the sailors lifted Slocum into the lighter as easily as if he had been a child.

"Thanks," he gasped and sprawled out full length on the planking, rubbing his leg and encouraging the pain to leave and normal feeling to return.

Above him he could hear excited shouts in Spanish. One of the Mexicans was throwing a vocal tantrum and waving a large knife through the air. The other two continued to glare down into the boat. Then, as one, the three turned away and began to race off down the wharf. Their anger did not give Slocum the idea that they had given up on the notion of getting their hands on him.

"Friends of yours?"

"Real sudden acquaintances, anyhow," Slocum said.

"I think they want you to come back for a spell."

"Just a short visit."

The sailor grunted. "Well, since you wasn't trying to sink us, an' believe me that seemed in doubt right at the first, I 'spect you're free to gᵔ ashore an' talk to them all you want."

"I, uh, wouldn't really mind if you were to let me off over on the other side of the harbor," Slocum said. "I have . . ." His voice died away as he felt for the pocket of his trousers and realized that his money belt was back in that room. He did *not* have anything to pay for his fare.

Come to think of it, he reflected, his money belt probably was long gone from the hotel room, too. Undoubtedly, by now the girl, whoever she was, had found it and wandered off with it.

Bitch, Slocum thought. Good in the sack but still a bitch.

"You was saying?" the sailor prompted.

Slocum shook his head. "I seem to've been cleaned out."

Several of the oarsmen chuckled; that wouldn't be a thing they were unfamiliar with themselves. But the man who seemed to be in charge shrugged. "Bad luck, mate, but we got work to do. No pay, no passage; that's the name of the game."

"I can't pay."

"Then it's been lovely knowin' you, mate, but out you go."

One of the oarsmen laughed and pointed toward the landward end of the wharf. "Your timing ain't great today, fella."

Slocum looked where the man was pointing. There in a small dinghy came two of the Mexicans. The third remained on the wharf with Slocum's pistol cocked and ready.

At least, Slocum reflected, the trio did not seem to want to take on this whole boatload of sailors in addition to their primary target. They were still hopping mad but were not shooting toward the lighter. Which it seemed Slocum was going to have to vacate, voluntarily or otherwise.

"There is another choice, mate," the boss sailor said. "Interested?" He was grinning. Slocum was already under the impression that this option might not be one he would like.

"I'll listen to most anything," Slocum told him.

"You see that ship ridin' at anchor out there?" He hooked a thumb toward a smallish sailing vessel lying with its sails furled perhaps a quarter mile away. Even from the distance the craft had a ratty look about it. Slocum nodded.

"We're on our way back aboard, y' see, an' we happen to be a trifle shorthanded. We could use another man in the crew." He grinned again. "Or we could bid ya hail an' farewell and return ya to the attentions of your, uh, acquaintances over there."

Slocum had to chew on that for only the briefest of moments. If he had even had his Bowie on his belt it would have been different. But that finely balanced weapon had been attached to his gun belt along with the Colt that was now in hostile hands. It seemed he had damned little to choose from in the situation.

"Boys," he said, "I have always wanted to be a sailor. See the ocean blue. All that crap." His voice was somewhat more doleful than the words.

The boss sailor laughed. "Then welcome aboard, swab. You'll never have a moment's regret."

Slocum sighed. He doubted the accuracy of the man's statement. On the other hand, if he didn't accept their generous offer, John Slocum was likely to have damned few moments left in which to regret anything.

"Bear a hand, swab, on that sweep o'er there."

"Sweep?"

"Oar, you fuckin' idiot. That long dingus that makes us go somewheres. Grab hold of the fucker an' pull."

"Aye aye," Slocum mumbled. He meant the expression as a joke but none of the sailors seemed to notice.

Already Slocum was beginning to wonder if he had accepted the greater of the evils here.

With four pairs of sweeps pulling, the lighter began to move slowly offshore toward the waiting ship.

With any luck, Slocum thought, and John Slocum's luck was damned near legendary, that ship out there was on its way down the coast to Brownsville. And *that* would be all *right*.

5

"Florida!!?? Shee-it." Slocum was disgusted. And busy. The boatswain—whatever that was; it was what they called the boss sailor who had been in the lighter, and Slocum gathered that it was about the equivalent of a sergeant in a more understandable form of rank—had not been lying when he said the ship was undermanned. There were only five sailors in addition to Slocum, and it seemed like it required more hands than all of them possessed just to get the sails set. At the moment, he was clinging to a rope perch some twenty-odd feet above the surface of the deck, trying at the same time to keep himself from falling and to follow a series of vulgar but otherwise almost incomprehensible orders that made no sense at all to his landbound background.

The ship was called the *Amalie*, and Slocum could already comprehend that she was a bit of a pig among ships. She was ill cared for and, for all Slocum knew, unsafe and overloaded. Certainly she did not move with any particular vigor when finally they got the sails set and began to gather in some wind for motive power. The breeze filled the sails and the little ship groaned and creaked and began to wallow off from the Texas coastline.

Which was all right, except that their destination was some hellhole of a place called Florida. A helluva distance from Brownsville, if Slocum remembered correctly. He had known a few men from that far-off section during the war, and as far as he could remember, he had not been much impressed. None of them had ever spoken fondly of home.

The boatswain, named McClain but called mister by

the crew, said the *Amalie* made regular runs between Cedar Key and Rockport, hauling cedar timber in one direction and returning with green hides and barrels of tallow.

It was a bitch of a way to make a living, as far as Slocum could tell.

The captain of the *Amalie* was a reed-thin and austere figure in a long-tailed frock coat who might have looked distinguished if it had not been for the telltale red veining in his over-large nose. The only name Slocum had heard the man called so far was Captain.

The first, and only, mate, which Slocum equated to a lieutenant, was named Bowder, but he too was called mister.

Slocum had not bothered to sort out the crew's names. He did not intend to be among them long enough to care what the poor bastards were called.

At the moment he was really too busy to think or care about much of anything except preserving his neck from death by falling. Trotting around on a strand of hemp slung high over the deck of a ship was not exactly John Slocum's idea of a good time.

Eventually, more in spite of his help than because of it, the bosun was satisfied with the set of the sails, and the captain went below decks, leaving the helm to the first officer and the crew to their own devices.

"Slocum!"

"Aye," Slocum bellowed. It still sounded like some kind of joke to him, but it was the way all the rest of the men responded. Down on firm planking again at last, he trotted over to where the bosun was waiting with his hands on his hips and a glare on his face.

"You're one sorry sonuvabitch of a sailor, mate," the bosun greeted him.

"I told you I'd always wanted to run away to the ocean blue," Slocum said. "I never told you I knew a damn thing about it."

"It don't take no kinda genius to figure that out, but you're a swab now an' a swab you'll stay until the cap'n tells you otherwise. I'll expect you to pull your share o' the work.''

"That I can give you.''

"Damn right you will, or the cap'n will have you flogged.''

It would be a hell of a trick if they could pull that off, Slocum thought. They could kill him if they worked at it. Any man can be taken down. But there were not enough men on this or a dozen other damned ships to put a lash to John Slocum's back.

The bosun might have seen something of that response in Slocum's dark, flashing gaze, because the man looked away and seemed to swallow back whatever else he might have been going to add.

"You're on the first watch an' the third," the bosun informed him. "All hands turn to as needed, regardless o' the watch order. Crew's quarters is in the fo'c'sle. Which you prob'ly don't know is up in the front part o' the vessel. But if you think you get to laze about in your hammock half the day an' all the night you're in for a rude awakenin'. Now lay below to the galley an' help Perkins stow the victuals. After that I want you t' help him with the cookin'. If you hear an 'all hands' call, you drop whatever you're doin' and come a-running. Understand me?''

Slocum grinned. He couldn't help himself. "Practically none of it,'' he answered quite honestly.

The bosun looked like he would like to hit Slocum. Instead he spit. And repeated the orders in English.

"Whatever you say, sergeant,'' Slocum said. He went off, feeling somewhat better, to look for the stairs—ladder—that allegedly led down to the galley—kitchen.

"Slocum.''

"Mmmm?''

"You awake?''

"I'm afraid so.'' Slocum was dog-tired, not just from the work he had been doing but much more from the constant shifting of balance and muscle as he adjusted to the movements of the rolling ship. He was unaccustomed to such activity, and it bothered him.

Yet as tired as he was after standing first watch, and knowing as he did that he would have to be back on deck in four short hours, he had been unable to slip into restful sleep.

He was stretched out in a hammock instead of a cot or even a rock-lumpy bedroll, which he would have found comfortable enough, and the damned hammock felt decidedly insecure as it swayed to the motions of the ship.

The fo'c'sle stank too, of sweat and mildew and urine and a thousand other unidentifiable odors.

Worst of all, Slocum's unconscious hearing, tuned to warn him of the dangers of approaching men or wildlife or whatever, was anything but adjusted to the constant sounds of a ship at sea.

Every slat of a sail or creak of plank or hum of wind-taut rope brought him alert to an unknown danger.

If this kept up, he knew, he was going to be one sad son of a bitch before too many days were gone.

Tired as he was, though, the voice he recognized as that of Perkins, the sailor/cook of the stinking *Amalie*, was almost welcome.

Slocum sat up, momentarily lost his balance to the immediate shift of the hammock, and damn near fell onto the floor. Deck. Whatever. As far as Slocum was concerned it was and could damn well remain a floor. Fuck a bunch of nautical crap. This life was not his and never would be.

"What do you want, Perkins?"

A shadowy form materialized beside him in the darkness of the fo'c'sle. There was not enough light to see the man's features, but the huge bulk indicated that it would be Perkins. The man was built like a grizzly and was fully capable of handling a hogshead cask of flour by himself. Slocum might not have believed that had he not seen it for himself earlier in the day, when the two of them were storing the ship's supplies in the galley.

"You aren't a man that knows the sea, Slocum," Perkins whispered.

"An' here I thought I had you all fooled," Slocum said.

Perkins chuckled, and Slocum could visualize the expression tucked in amid the grizzle of a graying beard stubble and a network of scars that creased the sailor's flat-nosed, salt-cured face. Almost hidden in the stubble, Perkins had a tattoo on both sides of his neck: the hilt of a dagger under one ear and a knife tip with bright red dripping blood beneath the other. It was not a decoration Slocum could find much favor in, but Perkins seemed quite proud of it.

"There's a few things you should know," Perkins said.

Slocum waited for him to go on. He thought he could hear some ropes creaking nearby that might mean the other man on their watch, named Mallory, was also awake and listening, but Slocum was not yet sure of his hearing in these surroundings.

"Shipmates generally watch out for each other," Perkins went on. "Protect each other, like. Do favors back an' forth. You know what I'm talking about?"

Slocum shook his head, realized it was too dark for the answer to have been seen, and said, "I don't reckon I do."

"What I'm saying is, shipmates oughta be close to one another. 'Specially watchmates. Protect each other from them bastards in the other watch. Or look out, say, for ol' Mallory over there. What I'm saying is, I'm offerin' to keep ol' Mallory offa your back."

Slocum thought he could hear Mallory snicker. And no wonder. Mallory was approximately half Perkins's size, a wiry little man who could swarm up a ratline as quickly and as easily as Slocum could run up a small mound on solid ground and who could swing hand over hand along the lines as readily as a monkey. It was not exactly likely that Slocum would need protection from Mallory, though, even if the smaller man had a cutlass and a belaying pin to make an attack with. Anyone that size John Slocum could swat like a mosquito.

"That's damned decent of you, I'm sure," Slocum said.

"You bet it is, pretty man," Perkins said. Slocum could hear the low, furry sound of a laugh from him. "An' the truth is, I seen you this evening when you took a piss off the rail. I'd say you're the best-hung swab on this here ship."

"An honor, I'm sure." Slocum sighed and shifted his weight on the flimsy hammock, gathering himself and trying to set himself in readiness for what he expected to come next.

He shook his head. All those stories the troops used to tell with such glee about sailors. Turned out they weren't as full of shit as Slocum had thought.

"So the way it's gonna be, sweetie . . ." Perkins was saying.

Slocum launched himself for the spot where he thought that tattoo should be.

6

They crashed together into the timber-ribbed bulkhead that was the ship's hull, and Slocum could feel the impact reach him through Perkins's massive body.

It was a hell of a powerful jolt, but Perkins seemed unaffected. He was no stranger to rough-and-tumble, that was certain. The big man clenched his fists together and formed a wedge with his forearms. He jammed the wedge with awesome strength between Slocum's wrists and broke Slocum's grip on his neck.

As soon as the contact was lost, Slocum rolled aside and came to his feet in a crouch, ready to defend himself or to attack as the opportunity came.

Perkins had size and strength on his side of the contest, and he had as well a strong advantage in that he was used to the shifting footing aboard the ship while Slocum was not.

The only thing Slocum could think of that might be turned to his advantage was the fact that the fo'c'sle was in near-darkness. Only a faint glow of moonlight came through the open hatch overhead. Both men were nearly blind, but Slocum believed that he had an edge in quickness over the bigger man.

The question now was how to use it.

Perkins was no more than a shadow in front of Slocum's eyes. Black against near-black. He was moving now. Slocum could see the shadow glide to his right.

Give credit where it's due, Slocum told himself. And take warning, too. For such a large man, Perkins moved well. His bare feet passed over the plank deck without so much as a whisper of sound. If Slocum ever lost him

31

in the darkness there could be hell to pay, because it might not be possible to hear Perkins.

Slocum crabbed sideways to his left, trying to position himself so Perkins would be between him and the uncovered hatch, giving himself as much of an advantage as would be possible in that poor light.

He saw, or thought he saw, Perkins's right fist lash out, and Slocum flicked a forearm up to block it.

The punch had been a fake, as Slocum realized too late. Before he could recover, Perkins had stepped in closer and hooked a low, vicious left into Slocum's belly, catching him just below the belt buckle and driving deep.

Slocum gasped, but he was already spinning away. A meaty right hand grabbed the air where Slocum's throat had just been.

The bastard was quick, dammit, Slocum thought. Quicker than a man that size had any right to be.

Slocum dodged and shuffled away, cautious of his footing and wary now about Perkins's abilities. But now Slocum had lost that slim advantage of position in the faint glimmer of moonlight. And Perkins knew the interior of the fo'c'sle far better than John Slocum ever would.

Perkins glided forward, silent as a ghost. Slocum sank down on his haunches and waited, watching the flow of the shadow before him, gathering his muscles like so many steel cables, knowing this was a fight he dared not lose.

Perkins was close now. He cocked his head to the side, and Slocum thought the big sailor might be having trouble seeing Slocum in the shadows.

Slocum flung his left hand high into the air. As he had hoped, the movement caught Perkins's eye, and his chin lifted to follow the half-seen motion.

Slocum slashed out with his right hand held flat like the blade of a hatchet. The hard side of his hand caught Perkins in the throat, and Slocum followed immediately with a swift slice of his foot into Perkins's crotch. Perkins went down with a grunt of pain.

The temptation was to press the attack now that Perkins was down, but Slocum held back. The big bastard was too tough to let himself be taken that easily, Slocum was sure. He was in pain, but he was still able to fight, and Slocum wanted no part of wrestling with a man that size. He backed off.

Perkins came to his feet again. Quickly and easily. He had been faking at least part of that fall. Slocum had been right to stay away from him.

They circled each other in the cramped space of the crew's quarters, both men breathing heavily now, intent on their combat. The sounds of their breathing made an eerie counterpoint to the groanings of the ship under way. Except for that, though, they fought in silence. There were neither curses nor threats.

Behind him Slocum could hear movement, a sound of bare feet striking the deck and scurrying away. Mallory. Getting the hell out of the way, Slocum thought. He heard Mallory scuttle topside up the short ladder. Slocum did not look in that direction. His attention was focused completely on the shadowy form of Perkins.

Perkins moved in on him again, and Slocum gave ground cautiously. The big man was very close again.

Slocum faked another kick to draw Perkins's attention, then stabbed his extended knuckles toward Perkins's face, trying for the eyes.

His knuckles struck the solid bone of Perkins's forehead instead, and the impact hurt like hell. His hand would be sore for days, Slocum knew, and it was just as well that he wouldn't have to face anyone in a gunfight during that time. A split knuckle could make the difference between life and death then.

On the other hand, Slocum wished he had his revolver in his hand right now. That would solve the problem.

But then if he had his Colt, back in Rockport, he wouldn't be in a stinking ship's fo'c'sle this moment, scrapping for his damned virginity. Of sorts.

It was a bitch of a position for a man to be in. Made Slocum wonder if women ever felt this way.

Perkins paused in the slow, circling dance they had been doing. It was enough to give Slocum warning.

Perkins threw himself forward, obviously intending to batter Slocum to the deck. And once down and locked together there was little doubt that the much larger man could prevail.

Slocum darted sideways. He leaped away but left his leg extended. Perkins struck Slocum's leg at knee level and spilled forward.

For the first time the big man bawled out aloud, not a word so much as an inarticulate cry of rage.

That was the last sound Perkins made for some time. The fo'c'sle was tiny and cluttered with hammocks and sea chests. Perkins was tipped forward by the trip and already was moving rapidly in his dive. He took a rapid step forward, but there was no room in which he might recover his balance. Headfirst, he crashed into the bulkhead with a monstrously loud, dull thud.

Slocum heard it and winced. He hoped the hull was intact after that. Hell, a ram could hardly do better.

He thought about finding a lantern and lighting it to see if Perkins's brains were slopping up the already dirty floor.

On the other hand, John Slocum did not particularly *care* if Perkins's brains had been spilled.

From above, Slocum heard the first officer call out for the third watch to come topside, and a moment later he could hear the approach of bare feet as the men on the other watch hurried back toward their hammocks. Slocum headed for the ladder. One of the others could rouse Perkins if they wanted to. And if they were able to. Or throw the bastard overboard if he was dead.

Slocum reached the clean, fresh, salt-scented air on deck and took a deep breath. At least up here the light was stronger and he could see to defend himself if Perkins was still in a mood to make trouble.

Or any other sonuvabitch, for that matter.

Slocum found himself wishing for a quick passage. To any damn place. It didn't have to be Brownsville. Anywhere would do, including the many anywheres where there were wanted posters out for a tall, lean, dark man named John Slocum.

In the meantime, though, there was a lousy ship to be sailed. Slocum sucked on his split knuckles and moved aft toward Mallory and the first officer.

7

There were some things that Slocum did not *want* to learn about the sailing of a ship. And others that he simply could not comprehend, like their fool system of bells in order to tell time. He decided quickly that it was easier to listen for the cussing and follow the lead of the others rather than try to decipher the frequent ding-a-ling crap.

There were a few other things that Slocum truly would have liked to learn. Like how in the hell a man was supposed to get any sleep on board the *Amalie* when a creep like Perkins was on the same watch.

The second night out Slocum took the precaution of gingerly getting into his hammock with a belaying pin for company. It was just as well that he did. Before he had a chance to get comfortably settled into sleep, Perkins was back, this time with a dirk in his hand. His intentions were obvious, but a backhanded slash with the belaying pin discouraged him.

On the other hand, Slocum knew he couldn't expect to defend himself day and night for the week or so it would take for the passage to Florida. He was bone-weary beat from the hard work to begin with and from the lack of rest, and constant vigilance was too much to ask on top of that.

Under other circumstances the problem wouldn't have been of any consequence. Break the fucker's neck and wander off to elsewhere. But these were not normal circumstances, and where can a man run to if he's trapped on a floating piece of shit in the middle of the Gulf of Mexico. No place, Slocum concluded. He had to leave Perkins alive. At least for the time being.

On the other hand, he damned well had to get some sleep. He resolved that, more or less, on the third night by slipping away from the others at the conclusion of his watch and sneaking below decks into the cargo hold, which, surprisingly to Slocum, the sailors seemed to regard as nonexistent. Their world consisted of the deck and rigging, galley and fo'c'sle. And that was all.

The hold was filled with bales of hides and barrels of tallow, both of which stank. However, there was no Perkins there, and Slocum curled up with a reasonable degree of contentment on top of one of the hide bales to wait for the next watch order. He had slept in worse places and with worse smells before, and he thought for the first few minutes that he was home free.

Then he discovered otherwise with skin-crawling suddenness.

A thin scrabble of sound alarmingly close to his ear brought him alert, and he automatically grabbed for his belaying pin with the thought that Perkins had somehow crept up on him down in this unlikely place.

He touched not hard, use-polished wood, though, but live, moving fur.

And then he felt tiny, clawed paws scurry over his wrist.

Jesus!!!

Slocum was barely able to choke back the yell that leapt to his throat unbidden.

Rats! There was a herd of fucking rats in the hold of the ship.

They were crawling all over.

He could *feel* them.

Slocum kicked at them, swept them off the bale with his arms, grabbed the belaying pin, and flailed out in all directions in the darkness.

John Slocum detested rats. Couldn't stand the filthy little sons of rat bitches. Now he was surrounded by them.

He swung his legs down from the bale and his heel

came down on one's head. He could hear the crunch of broken bone.

Thank goodness he had come down on the head instead of the haunches or the little bastard would have sunk its teeth into Slocum's bare foot for sure. He hopped briefly on the other foot, feeling distinctly unclean. It was a strange sensation and an ugly one, and Slocum's first inclination was to run.

But the only other place he could think of to go would be back to his hammock and that damned Perkins's dementia. If he did that, Slocum knew good and well he would end up killing the prick. He would have no choice about it. And while that would be no particular loss or cause for regret, the consequences out on a damned ship where there was no chance for escape made the prospect unappealing.

And he *had* to get some sleep.

Finally, shakier than any fight with an entire mob of men could have made him, Slocum calmed his breathing and forced himself to think.

He lighted a candle he had stolen from the galley earlier and sat on a bale where he could watch for the approach of any more of the darkly horrible little creatures. He held the belaying pin clutched in a ready fist, but at least for the time being they seemed to be repelled by the light.

Light, of course, would be no permanent answer. The rats would soon enough become accustomed to it, and that would be the end of Slocum's sleep once again.

The only other thing he could think of . . . He grinned and made his way across the piled bales to the far side of the hold, where the barrels of tallow were stacked.

A moment to tip a barrel onto its side, a few kicks from a powerful leg, and that should solve the problem.

The little bastards were hungry? Fine. They could wallow in all the tallow they wanted to eat. If that barrel ran empty he could break open another. None of the crew would see the damage until they unloaded the cargo, and by that time John Slocum expected to be long gone from the *Amalie* and all who were connected with her. Slocum did not care if the ship reached port with the whole stinking hold empty except for a herd of overfed rats. And he did care about sleep.

He tilted the barrel up to make sure plenty of the whitish glop oozed out onto the deck and then made his way, much more cheerfully, back to the far side of the hold. He blew out the candle, stretched out, and for the first time since he had awakened beside that pretty little Mexican bitch fell into a sound sleep.

"The point is, one passage I'll give you, just for the transportation. But by damn I expect to be paid for my work coming back the other way. I told you already I got to get down to Brownsville. An' I ain't afraid of work. But you'll pay me or I'll find another ship to sail on. An' that's the way she sets, podner." Slocum had his jaw set in a firm jut, and he had no intention of being told otherwise.

"You're on my ship now," the bosun began, "an'—"

"And that's my point entirely," Slocum insisted. "If you want me to sign on for the return voyage, you'll damn well pay me just the same as you do every other member of this crew. You pay me, I'm on your ship; you want to shag me for another free ride and I'm one gone sonuvabitch. There's other ships on this duck pond, some of them going straight to Brownsville. So you make up your mind, mister, and let me know. But I don't work pointing west without you pay me."

The argument had been going on for two days already, and Slocum was as firm now as when it had started. They were less than a day out of port, according to the first officer, and Slocum wanted the issue settled.

Actually, what he wanted was for the bosun and the officers to *think* it was settled.

John Slocum was still barefoot and living in only the pair of trousers he had pitched out of that window with.

If they were expecting him to jump ship in Cedar Key they would be watching him closely, and Slocum would rather they be assured he was still their boy.

Which was a bunch of bullshit. What with Perkins and the rats and the almost inedible food and the lack of sleep, there was no way in hell or out that John Slocum would be sailing on the stinking *Amalie* again.

Besides, once that hold was opened and the cargo unloaded, somebody was going to be highly pissed off. Slocum had been kicking open a fresh barrel of tallow every night, and the profits from this voyage were not going to be what the captain expected.

The bosun grumbled more at some length, but they were already in sight of land, and the bastard wanted to make sure of his crew. He finally gave in to Slocum's demands.

"Ye'll draw a reg'lar wage then, damn ye. But I'll be expectin' to see the sweat fly off'n your hide every league o' the way."

"Aye aye," Slocum snapped smartly. He trotted off with every outward sign of diligence. But what he was *thinking* would have made the bosun's blood run cold.

They reached port just before dark and anchored offshore, as they had done back in Rockport.

"We unload come mornin'," the bosun said. "Meantime there's a watch to be kept aboard."

"I'll do it," Slocum volunteered. "I got no money to blow ashore anyhow."

Perkins gave him a dark look that said he was hoping Slocum would have been in the shore party too, but the others looked relieved. None of them had any desire to be stuck on board the *Amalie* when there were bars and women—or boys if their preferences ran that way—so near.

The bosun grunted, and Slocum guessed that he would have been the one given the watch even if he had not volunteered for it. The bosun had little enough reason to trust him to return to the ship, even after several days of argument about a wage.

A lighter came out from the town, the lights of which Slocum could see across a quarter mile of calm water. The captain went through some formalities that Slocum did not care enough to watch, and the lighter drew away with the crew and officers hitching a ride in it. Only Slocum and the bosun stayed aboard.

"I'll be goin' below," the bosun said when the others were gone. "See that you keep the lanterns burnin' lest some idiot of a fisherman ram us in th' dark. If ye need me, give out a yell; I'll hear ye."

Slocum nodded and found himself a seat on a hatch cover.

The night air was close and cloyingly hot. Sweat ran down Slocum's bare chest, and he wished unsuccessfully for a breeze that might give an impression of coolness. He wished just as unsuccessfully for a breath of mountain air with the sharp, tangy scent of snowmelt in it. This was not country that John Slocum liked, and he cursed the fates that had brought him here. It was a bitch, he decided without ever seeing it.

He waited patiently to give the bosun time to fall asleep or get himself drunk or whatever he was doing below decks. Eventually Slocum came to his feet and padded silent and barefoot toward officer's country, which he had never seen despite the length of time he had been on the ship.

No hatch and ladder for the gentlemen—so to speak— of the ship; they had a real door and a set of stairs down into their quarters. There was a lantern illuminating the passageway. Another light showed beneath the door of one cabin. That would be the bosun's.

Slocum entered the first cabin he came to. It was a disappointment: tiny and cramped and smelling very nearly as bad as the fo'c'sle Slocum had learned to hate. He recognized a cap hung on a peg as belonging to the first mate. It was the captain's cabin he wanted.

He took a quick look down the passageway. There was neither sight nor sound of the bosun. The bastard hadn't been that bad to him, Slocum had already decided, and if he could leave without doing the man any harm he would do so. If not . . . that would be the bosun's problem.

An even smaller cubbyhole, presumably intended for a second officer the *Amalie* did not carry, was being used for charts and storage.

Finally he found the captain's quarters, closed the door behind him, stuffed the captain's best dress uniform down at the crack over the sill so no light would show through, and lighted a candle. Slocum began to grin.

Ten minutes later, dressed except for the boots he carried in one hand, and armed with a pair of knives and an elderly but deadly-looking single-shot horse pistol, John Slocum took his leave of the good ship *Amalie* and rowed himself to shore in the ship's dinghy.

8

This was odd country indeed, Slocum thought. It smelled dank and half rotten. The shacks—they didn't qualify for the term "building," in Slocum's estimation—were crudely fashioned of clapboard and scrawny logs. There were no boardwalks along the storefronts. Even the ground underfoot felt odd: soft and spongy, without the firmness one expects from good, solid earth.

Still, there are some things that don't seem to change. He had no trouble at all in identifying the area he wanted, which was a line of shanties that were saloons and raggedy-assed cathouses. Those a man could always recognize from sound and smell regardless of their odd appearance here.

Slocum wandered slowly through the shadows, enjoying the sense of freedom he got from being shut of the miserable ship back in the harbor.

The captain owned—used to own—a floppy-brimmed slouch hat along with his collection of uniform caps, and this now sat atop Slocum's finely molded head, the brim drooping low to largely conceal his dark good looks. He doubted that any of the crew from the *Amalie* would have recognized him if he had passed them in full daylight, accustomed as they were to seeing him in reeking pants and sunburnt skin alone. At night, with only an occasional spill of distant lamplight to illuminate the dust that passed for a street here, he was sure none of them would know him if they walked right into him. And that was just fine.

He idled along the fronts of the bars and the cribs with a casual confidence that told anyone who looked that he was a gentleman out to get a glimpse at how the lower orders lived.

The truth was that he had no money to go into any of the dives and order so much as a beer. But thanks to the captain's choice in civilian clothing, no onlooker could have guessed as much.

Slocum took his time about his stroll, stopping to peer into every window without haste before he drifted on. Eventually he saw what he had been looking for. And began to chuckle. There he stayed, watching silently, for some time.

"Unngh. Uh." There was the deep rumble of a monumental belch, and a moment later the flimsy door of the four-holer swung open with a shriek of unoiled protest on its hinges. A massive pair of shoulders blocked the light and the door swung shut.

Perkins had already unbuckled his belt and was fumbling with the buttons at his fly. His sighs indicated he was already prepared for a soul-satisfying dump.

"Good evenin', bunkie," came a voice out of the darkness.

"Huh?"

"I said good evening."

"Yeah, sure." There was a sound of trousers falling to the board floor with a soft plop of cloth, then the creak of overburdened wood.

"I've been waiting to have a word with you," the voice came again. "Kinda thought it ought to be in private."

"Huh? What kind of crap is this?"

There was a faint sound of sniffing. "Rather nasty, actually. You should watch what you eat, Perkins. Anybody smells that bad it might mean there's something wrong with his insides."

"Who the fuck are you, anyhow? And what's this about my insides? Man, I don't know who you are, but I'm beginnin' to think I don't like you. Go 'way."

"What, after I waited all this time for you? I don't think so." The voice laughed softly.

There was a quality in the sound of the laughter that brought a chill to Perkins's spine. He had not been alarmed by man nor storm in many years. He felt the first stirrings of alarm now.

"Who *are* you?" His voice reflected what he was feeling, and he did not like the sound. That made him angry, and that was to the good. He knew how to deal with anger. Anger turned so swiftly, so sweetly, to rage. And rage he knew full well how to vent on whatever unfortunate sonuvabitch was handy. Rage he could always find an outlet for.

The voice laughed again.

"Little man"—to Perkins very nearly all other men were regarded as little—"I don't know who the fuck you are, but I think when I'm done crapping here I'm gonna see if you can swim. An' your first lesson is gonna be in this here outhouse pit. You get me? You know what I'm sayin' to you?"

The response was another of those spine-chilling laughs. Perkins did not like the sound of that laugh. It made his skin crawl worse than the lice in his blankets ever had. Whoever this bastard was he should be scared shitless by now. That laugh did not sound the least bit afraid. Anything but.

Perkins reached for his dirk, realized that his pants were in a puddle of cloth around his ankles and bent over to gain the comforting assurance of having the slim, ugly weapon balanced in his palm.

"Uh-uh. Naughty boy."

There was a touch, a whisper-soft touch, at his throat. Perkins felt the hair at the back of his neck stiffen as he tensed. He knew without having to feel its bite that the feather-light touch came from a sharply honed blade. Perkins's bowels evacuated with a rush.

"A mite nervous, Perkins? Sounds like it."

There was that laugh again. Perkins shivered.

"Who are you???" The question came out in a quavering wail.

"I'll confess it to you, Perkins old son. I'm not a friend of yours."

"Oh, Jeez," Perkins moaned.

"Nope. Wrong guess."

Perkins tried to turn his head, wanting desperately to look into the deep shadow that filled the outhouse. The first hint of movement brought a tightening of the slight pressure against his throat, and he thought he could feel a trickle of warm, fresh blood seep down his throat into the hair that matted his chest. He sobbed aloud in spite of himself. He hadn't been so terrified since he first shipped as a cabin boy and discovered for the first time what was expected of him in that position.

"It isn't good for a grown man to cry," the voice told him. "I'll tell you what, old son. How's about if I offer you a way out of this mess you've gotten into. Would you like that?"

Perkins began to nod, felt the knife, and thought better of it. He managed a croak that more or less resembled a guttural yes.

"Say again?"

Perkins steeled himself, licked dry lips, and tried again. "Yes. I said yes. I'd like a way out. Jesus."

There was that laugh. Perkins shuddered. He would have nightmares about that laugh for the rest of his life. If he had any more life to live.

"I told you once already," the voice said, "I ain't him. An' unlike him, ol' buddy ol' pal, I got no compassion whatsoever." The knife blade tightened fractionally against Perkins's throat, and this time he was certain he could feel a warm flow of blood. He squinted his eyes tightly closed, as if that would make the bogeyman go away.

"You said . . . ?" The rest of what he wanted to say trailed off into a gurgle.

"Oh, yes. The way out. Well, I've been thinking about that, Perkie ol' boy. And I did have something in mind. But you gave me a better idea yourself. Just a minute or so ago. I thank you for it.''

Perkins turned his head cautiously toward the unseen stranger, toward the voice. The blade followed his slight movement as if it had become a part of his skin.

"You're asking me what this better idea was, is that it?'' The voice chuckled. The chuckle was very nearly as bad as the laugh.

"Uh.'' It was all he could manage.

"A swim, ol' pal. I think that's the way you put it. A little moonlight swim. Convenient too. Practically right where you're sitting.''

Perkins sobbed.

"Now, now, Perkie, you don't have to get all choked up with gratitude. I know how much you 'preciate it. That's enough for me.'' The voice hardened. "Well?''

"Whatever you say. Sure.''

He said it too easily, though. Too readily. The quick acquiescence was too sudden for a man who had lived a life as hard as Perkins had, and there was a note of falseness in it.

Perkins had learned survival in a rough, saltwater school, in the stink and the sodomy of half a hundred ships, and his experience had always been that it was the other man who had to bow to Perkins's strength and Perkins's experience. And now, finally, he was beginning to feel the steel form in his backbone.

That voice. Piss on the voice and the man who owned it, Perkins thought. Let him think Perkins was giving in to him. Let him believe he had won. The belief would not last long.

And when he knew otherwise, it would be Perkins's knife that flooded the boards of the outhouse floor with slippery, copper-smelling blood, and the bastard, whoever he was, would find that the crapper had become a grave. And wouldn't Perkins like the thought of *that* come tomorrow's dawn.

Perkins's lips drew back in a wolflike grin. He flexed the immensely powerful slabbed muscles of his shoulders and arms. He would not even need his dirk. His bare hands would do the job unaided. Those hands had a grip that the vilest gale could never break, and his arms were capable of carrying even his immense weight hand over hand up a rigging with a rush that few men could follow.

All he needed was . . .

Perkins flung himself backward, away from the blade at his throat.

He bounced off the back wall of the outhouse, twisted his massive shoulders, and grabbed out with his powerful arms to encircle the owner of that voice, knowing, *knowing* that the man would expect him to roll away while in reality the crafty fighter would close with him, come inside the knife and break the bastard's back before he would ever know . . .

There was something wrong.

Perkins's arms were clamping down on . . . nothing. On nothing at all. *He wasn't there.*

The man had moved. Or he was no man at all. A ghost? That voice . . .

"Perkins? Naughty, naughty, ol' boy. But you have to admit, I *did* give you a chance."

The voice laughed.

Perkins felt sweat burst through his skin like ice water in the dank heat of the backhouse. He came to his feet, stumbled against the trousers that were still around his ankles, began to flail his arms wildly in all directions, trying to club the voice or to grapple with it.

He was in panic now. A stream of urine flooded down his left leg.

"I'll . . ."

He never finished whatever he might have said. From nowhere he felt the fiery bite of steel into flesh and then the even hotter boil of bright blood coursing from his severed throat. He squealed but could not speak.

"Tsk, tsk," the voice said. The sounds seemed to come from a very long way away.

The last thing Perkins saw was a flash of moonlight

coming through a crack high in the wall, a flash that caught in a man's eyes and was reflected there like a cold green flame.

Then the knife cut again, and Perkins knew no more. He never did come to know that his grave was a pit beneath an outhouse. Nor that that grave would never be discovered, for, after all, who in his right mind would ever want to look into, much less dig up, an old pit toilet. But of course Perkins was beyond caring anyway.

And the voice faded quietly away into the night.

9

"And old Tommy Lee, he come about that close to getting his nuts lopped off, 'cept o' course that little ol' gal couldn't tell her daddy on him without tellin' on herself too, so he . . ."

Slocum stifled a yawn and tried to at least register a polite expression in answer to the fellow's constant chatter. He had been talking nonstop ever since he gave Slocum a lift early that morning. And that had been hours ago. Slocum was beginning to wonder if the man would ever run out of things to say. He rather hoped that he would.

"Say now, I could use a bit of lunch. How 'bout yourself?"

That got through Slocum's disinterest. He hadn't eaten since the day before, back on the ship, and his belly felt as empty as those tallow barrels he had dumped. He was still cussing the *Amalie*'s captain for not being thoughtful enough to leave any cash lying about. Damned inconsiderate of him, actually.

"It sounds good, but . . ."

The teamster grinned and spat a brown stream of tobacco juice into the powdered sand that was the road-bed. "Broke, huh? I figured as much. No offense, mister, but, well, a man dressed like you an' havin' to bum a ride from a passing wagon, that kinda speaks of a long night with somebody else's cards. But, hell, I been there myself often enough. I calculate I can stand you to a bite."

"That's mighty kind of you," Slocum said. He meant it. He had been in places, and among people, where a hungry stranger was just shit out of luck.

The driver hauled on his lines and wheeled the pair of decrepit mules off the road to the shade of a monster-sized oak that had some strange, gray, hairy-looking stuff hanging in its limbs. The shade turned out not to provide any actual coolness, but at least it gave an illusion of relative comfort, and that was something. Slocum had long since gone beyond the point of misery in this incessant heat and was beginning to wonder if he was in danger of sweating away to the bare, white bones.

"Besides," the driver said with a spit and a grin, "what we're fixing to have for lunch don't cost anything."

Slocum raised an eyebrow, and the man hooked a thumb over his shoulder toward the tarp-covered wagon box behind them.

"That's what we're haulin' back there," the man said. "Food on the hoof, so to speak. Free, too. I pick 'em up around home time to time an' fling 'em in the back of the wagon. When I get enough I take 'em in to the quarters and sell 'em for a few cents each. It ain't much, but it's something, and I gotta make the trip in to town to buy victuals and such every so often anyhow."

Slocum nodded. "What is it you have back there then?"

Another spit, another grin. "Gophers." He used the back of his hand to wipe a dribble of the brown juice from his chin.

Slocum was not sure he had heard the fellow correctly. Then he decided he definitely had not heard correctly. Couldn't have. Gophers?

Aside from the fact that the little beggars looked like rats and probably were related to rats, why, there could not be a mouthful of meat on a dozen of them. And that was if someone was fool enough and strong-stomached enough to bring himself to eat a damned rodent.

"Gophers?" Slocum's expression reflected the opinion he had on the subject.

"Surest thing. You never tried 'em?"

"I cannot say that I have," Slocum said truthfully. The teamster was trying to be nice to him so he refrained from adding anything more.

"You're in for a treat," the man persisted. Slocum said nothing, but he had his own private opinion about it.

The driver hauled his mules to a halt and let them stand with slack rein while he hopped down to the ground. "If you'll build a fire, I'll do the rest," he said agreeably.

That much Slocum was willing to do. He dropped to the ground and began gathering likely-looking chunks from the deadwood that littered the ground. Much of it had some of that odd gray stuff still clinging to it in death, and Slocum paused to finger it. It had a dry, rubbery texture and was not very strong, strand by many-forked strand, although in quantity it had both strength and weight to it. Slocum searched back in his memory to the conversations he had overheard during the war years when boys from the Deep South had been talking. Some had spoken about missing the sight of moss in the trees. This, Slocum concluded, must be moss. He could not see anything so delightful in it that he would miss the sight. In fact, he would be delighted for an opportunity to get back onto the proper, western side of the Big Muddy and lose sight of this strange stuff.

Behind him the wagon driver had begun to chuckle.

"Something funny?" Slocum asked. There was a strong edge to the tone of his voice.

"Oh, don't get riled." The driver was aware of that edge but seemed unworried by its implied threat. This was indeed, Slocum reflected, a very different kind of country from anything he was used to. "I was just notin' that you ain't from around here anywheres."

"Yeah?"

"Uh huh," the man said pleasantly. "For one thing, you're lookin' at that there Spanish moss like it was somethin' weird. Which it ain't. For another, you're fingerin' it like you never heard o' redbugs."

"Redbugs? I'll bite, what are they?"

The man laughed. "Naw, mister, you ain't gonna be the one to do the biting. They are. That there moss is likely crawlin' with 'em."

Slocum turned the clump of gray stuff over in his hands. "I don't see any."

Again the wagon driver laughed. "Mister, I growed up in this country an' I can't say as I've ever seen one neither. But I've sure felt 'em. Too little to see. They get around a man's beltline or in his boots, anywhere. Kinda like chiggers except meaner. Got more of a taste for red meat."

Slocum dropped the moss as if it had suddenly caught fire. Chiggers he knew about from unpleasant experience. If these Florida redbugs were any worse than that, he wanted no part of them. He decided he had examined the Spanish moss all that he needed to and got about the business of building a fire, as his host had requested.

He got another surprise when the driver brought several large, gray land turtles out from under the wagon cover and began to butcher them ready for the fire.

"I thought you said we were going to have gophers for dinner," Slocum said.

"Reckon I did at that," the man agreed.

"But . . ." Slocum grinned, catching on finally. "That's a gopher, right?"

"O' course." The man shucked the breastplates and shells as easily as a mountain man would skin a rabbit.

"Shee-it," Slocum said. Turtle. Called gopher hereabouts. Well, there was nothing wrong with that. Some of the best eating possible was terrapin soup, and he was damn sure willing to give broiled turtle steaks a try. It beat eating a cousin to a rat any old time. But whoever would have thought that a turtle would be called by a rodent's name. He shook his head. There was a helluva lot he had to learn about this part of the country. Or not learn. He hoped to be shut of it before he would have a chance to learn much more.

There was, after all, still business to be done in Brownsville, back the other side of the Gulf of Mexico on soil Slocum could understand and appreciate. All John Slocum wanted from Florida was a way out of it.

10

Slocum found it funny as hell, although undoubtedly the sweating, cussing men involved were unable to find the least trace of humor in their situation.

The wagon Slocum was hitching a ride with had reached the crossroads first, but the driver was polite enough—or wise enough—not to interfere with the band of mounted, rough-looking men who were escorting a very heavily loaded freight wagon coming from another direction. The driver of the gopher wagon pulled to a stop, giving the others the right of way, and so Slocum had a ringside seat for the whole thing.

The big freight wagon was pulled by a six-up of huge, if unmatched, draft animals, but even so it was having difficulty negotiating the soft sand that passed for soil hereabouts. On the back of the freight wagon was a massive crate holding a dark red bull with short, polished horns. The bull looked almost as large as the draft horses that were pulling him in his odd conveyance, and Slocum wondered briefly why the fool cowboys hauling him didn't make the beast get out and earn his own keep by walking the rest of the way.

On the other hand, he was already discovering that there was an awful lot he didn't know about the way things were done here. For all Slocum knew they might also carry cows in carriages here. And it was none of his business to begin with.

In any event, the freight wagon reached the crossroads and swung into the turn onto the road in front of Slocum and his hospitable driver, but the leaders of the six-up did not swing quite wide enough and a back wheel rode up onto a hump of root lying next to the

road. The resulting jolt was enough to anger the bull.
And in an animal that size, a little anger is enough to
result in considerable damage.

The bull bawled once, snorted, and began to throw
his head back and forth, hooking the sides of the crate
with his stubby horns and working up a bellowing rage.

"That whole wagon's beginnin' to shake," Slocum's
seatmate said.

"Ain't it just," Slocum said with a grin. They could
hear a loud *crack* as overstressed wood gave way and
the side of the crate bulged. "An' I think it's fixing to
get worse."

Sure enough, the bull gave the crate a final shot with
its massive head and broke free. The animal stumbled
out of its confinement and promptly fell off the tailgate
of the wagon.

"Bright critters, these bovines," Slocum observed.

"Brighter than some people," the wagon driver said.
He too was grinning.

The freight wagon's escort by then had seen what
was going on and was in a dither of excitement, men
hauling at their horse's reins and whirling this way and
that, shouting orders and warnings to each other, getting into each other's way, none of them accomplishing
a thing as far as the now freed bull was concerned. That
animal came to his feet and began trying to hook his
horns into the clouds of dust that were swirling around
him. Ropy strands of snot flew in all directions. The
escort riders were still milling in circles shouting at
each other.

"I haven't seen so much activity since Aunt Minnie
set in an ant bed," Slocum said. "Course she was
under a handicap compared to these boys; she had to do
all the dancin' her own self."

The cowboys—at least Slocum *assumed* they were
trying to pass themselves off as cowboys, in spite of
being dressed in overalls and galluses and most of them
riding barefoot or the next thing to it—were beginning
to get themselves into some sort of order now. There

was less milling about and perhaps a little less shouting going on.

The bull had decided to ignore them. He shook himself and trotted off the dusty road toward a patch of tall, spindly looking trees where there would be the promise of some shade. Slocum watched him go and noted that those spindly trees seemed to be standing hip-deep in water, because the bull surely made some splashes when he went into them.

No wonder, Slocum thought. It would have been hot as hell inside that crate. The poor old bastard would be wanting to wallow now that he had found some moisture. Anything to cool off. Slocum considered joining him but decided against it. The big beef-maker was a bit too clever with his horns for that to be desirable.

"Goddamnit, somebody fetch me th' dogs. Who's got the damn dawgs?"

Slocum's attention returned to the cowboys who had been escorting the wagon. Now that they were holding still he could see that there were no more than half a dozen of them, and a beardless youngster on by far the best-looking horse of a poor bunch seemed to be doing all the hollering now.

"Where's the damn dawgs?" the kid bawled again.

"Here, Boyd," somebody said. A rider detached himself from the herd and moved over to the side of the wagon. He leaned down from his saddle and began to untie rope leashes from the collars of a pack of four unlikely looking curs that had been bedded down in the wagon in front of the crate. The cowboy, Slocum saw, was riding barefoot but had a pair of rusty spurs tied to his bare heels. The man's feet were filthy enough that it had taken Slocum a moment to determine that he was indeed both barefoot and wearing spurs. Slocum shook his head.

The dogs came spilling out of the wagon and began to bay, making the horses nervous and threatening to start the whole confusing process of impromptu rodeoing all over again.

"Get that damn bull back ovuh heah," the kid ordered no one in particular.

"Right, Boyd."

The other five riders formed up into a group that seemed to know what they were about, and one of them began snapping orders at the dogs. All the riders, Slocum saw, shook out not lariats but long, wicked-looking whips. The coils on their saddles were not ropes, as Slocum had been assuming without bothering to look closely, but bullwhips. There was not a catch rope in the crowd. Damned odd, Slocum thought.

"Reckon there's room to get past that idjit?" Slocum's driver asked.

"Actually I'm kinda enjoying watchin' this mess," Slocum said. The other man shrugged and reached into his shirt pocket for a chew. He left his driving lines lie, and the mules stood quietly grateful for the rest they were getting.

The cowboys and their dogs dashed across the short-grass flat beside the road and plunged into the stand of trees where the escaped bull had taken refuge. Sparkling water flashed in bright, sun-caught arcs around them as they entered the trees.

It was obvious what they intended. With the dogs nipping at the bull's heels and the cowboys driving him with their lashes they would move him back out into the open, force him back to the wagon, and—somehow—reload him into the broken crate aboard the wagon.

Except it didn't work quite like that.

For one thing, the bull was in no damned mood to be moved anywhere, by anybody or anything. For another, the water it was standing in was deep enough that the dogs could not get to its hocks unless they were willing to go underwater to do so. None of them seemed so inclined.

For another thing, at the first sting of the first cowboy's lash, the big bull sulled up. He shook his head with annoyance, but he didn't move. Instead he humped his back and tucked his tail low against his flank.

"That old sunuvabitch has decided he's had enough," Slocum said. "An' I'll bet there's no dog and no whip gonna move him neither. I've seen bovines sull up and die, just roll their eyes back in their heads and fall over dead before you could move them once they've sulled up like that."

The wagon driver spat and shrugged. Apparently he had little interest in the workings of the bovine mind.

The dogs were barking and splashing ineffectively around the sulled bull, and the cowboys moved in on horseback and began to slash him with their whips; but none of it so much as captured the bull's attention, much less getting him to quit the cool water and the shade he had found.

The kid the others were calling Boyd began yelling instructions again. "Dammit, boys, don't be hurtin' him. Papa'll give us all hell if you cut 'im up an' get 'im filled with screwworms. Shit, boys, you could ruin 'im. Don't *hurt* 'im."

"Hurt 'im," one of the cowboys yelled back. "Shit, Boyd, we cain't get his attention even. You want we should pick him up an' tote him back out there?"

"Dammit, boys, just don't hurt 'im. Jesus!" Boyd looked so sorrowful that Slocum could not help laughing out loud.

"What the fuck are you laughin' at, mistuh?" Boyd snapped nastily. "You want me to tell the boys t' put theah whips on yore ass next?"

"Oh," Slocum drawled happily, "I reckon anybody that figures he's man enough is welcome to try it. But I don't think that'd move your bull any more than those dogs and whips are already doing." He chuckled some more.

"I s'pose you think you could do better," Boyd snapped.

"Oh, I reckon I *could*. But then I got no call to, do I? Besides, this is so much fun watching that I'd hate to spoil the show." Slocum laughed again.

Boyd glared at Slocum, then turned back toward the

bull and his frustrated cowboys. "Bring 'im out now, boys."

"You bet, Boyd. Whatever you say."

Slocum thought the sound rather sarcastic, but he could not blame the cowboy under the circumstances.

There was a great deal more frenzied barking and the snappping of whips and a blue-smoke cloud of cussing coming out of those trees. But the bull stayed where he was.

"Dammit, I tol' you not to hurt 'im."

"Yeah, Boyd. Right. Whatever you say."

Slocum began laughing again.

"Goddamnit, mistuh, I tol' you to shut yore mouth."

Slocum laughed at him.

Boyd had colored up to a shade of red that made Slocum wonder if the kid was going to perish of apoplexy at his tender age. "Yore such a smart-ass, mistuh, you fetch 'im on out heah then."

"I told you once already," Slocum said softly, "I got no good reason to do that. And I'm having a whole lot of fun just sitting here."

"You want a reason? I'll give you a reason, mistuh. I got"—he dug into a shirt pocket—"I got a twen'y dollah gold piece heah that says you can't get 'im out. How's that fer a reason?"

"Are you serious, boy?"

"Damn straight I'm serious, mistuh. Twen'y dollahs if you can bring that theah animal t' the road. But if'n you cain't . . ."

"Oh, I can do it all right." Slocum grinned. "Climb down off that horse for a minute, son, and let me show you how they do it out in the big-grass country."

11

Getting the bull out of the trees and under control was the least of Slocum's worries. He generally preferred robbing banks to chasing cattle, on the theory that the former was both easier and better-paying than the latter, but he was perfectly capable of handling either task. And he was experienced in both.

He found a coil of limp hemp in the back of the wagon carrying the now empty shipping crate, and while it was much too soft to make a decent catch rope, it would do. He rode Boyd's horse—also too soft but suitable under the circumstances—to the edge of the motte and heeled two of the hounds with some practice loops so he could get the feel of the rope.

"Now boys," he said politely, "if you would take yourselves and those dogs off somewhere else, I will do what that youngster over there wants done."

The cowboys looked skeptical, but with some prodding from their underage boss they complied with Slocum's request.

Slocum nudged the horse into the swamp water with the bull and spoke a few of the words that bovines seem most likely to respond to. "C'mere you old sonuvabitch." The bull's ears twitched.

That was more like it. No longer surrounded by men and dogs and whips, the bull would no longer feel so threatened.

Slocum dropped a small loop over the animal's horns, took a wrap on the spindly horn that jutted up from Boyd's saddle, and backed away just enough to pull the bull's head around and force him to take a few sidesteps to retain his balance. Just enough to remind the stubborn beast that it had legs and was capable of using them. Slocum kicked the horse forward a step to loosen the pull on the rope and flipped his loop free of the horns. He rebuilt the wet rope into a coil and hung it on the saddle.

"Any ol' time now."

The bull twisted its head around to glare at him. But the animal had been reminded that it was free. And it was no longer surrounded by its enemies. There was only one it needed to escape from now.

As Slocum had hoped, the bull lowered its head and bawled once, whipped its tail into a curl over its massive haunches, and took off a-helling into a run out of the trees with branches snapping and dirty brown water spraying all around it.

"EEEeeeeeiiii-*hah*!!!" Slocum was after it at a dead run.

The bull broke onto the grass flat with Slocum and Boyd's horse right behind. Cowboys and dogs scattered to both sides, but neither the bull nor Slocum was paying them any mind.

Slocum spurred the horse hard and reined it savagely to force it close to the bull. The horse had never been asked to do work like this before and had to be manhandled into position.

Slocum placed himself beside the bull's hard-driving left hip. He was grinning when he bent from the saddle and grabbed hold of the bull's streaming tail. It had been a long time since he had performed this particular little maneuver himself. He was rather enjoying himself.

He yanked the tail up and took half a wrap around the horn with it, let out a short bark of a yell and hauled the horse hard to the left while he spurred it into a leap forward.

With its hind end suddenly and most unexpectedly snatched up and over, the bull, predictably, went a-tumble. It spilled scrotum-over-hornroot in a somersault and hit the ground in a dust-raising crash that knocked both the wind and the fight clean out of it.

Slocum, pleased with himself, hauled Boyd's excited horse into a sliding stop and turned to see what the bull was going to do next. With a tough old Texas longhorn or one of those feisty black Mexican bulls you sometimes had to knock them down two or even three times to teach them some manners.

But not this high-bred, easy-living, eastern-raised creature. Once was quite enough here.

"Reckon you should be able to drive him easy enough now," Slocum said to the worked-up youngster who had run up beside his stirrup. "But if I was you I wouldn't try an' reload the old bastard into that crate. An' I think I'd keep the dogs off'n him too. Just drive him easy and he shouldn't sull up on you again."

"Damnation, mistuh, I never seen nuthin' like that before. What d'ya call it anyhow?"

Slocum shrugged. "Tailing them down is all I've ever heard it called. Any good cowboy ought to be able to do it."

"Where you from, mistuh?" Boyd looked more excited than ever now. He was breathing hard, and Slocum did not believe that that little bit of a run from the wagon to the horse could have gotten him so far out of breath, not even if he was as soft as his horse.

Slocum shrugged. "All over. Anyplace there's grass or mountains. Mexico to Canada and all the places in between, I been there, son. Couldn't exactly say that I'm *from* any of them, but you could make a case for me being from *all* of them if you wanted."

"Jesus. Oh, Jesus. Are you a for-real western cowboy, mistuh?"

Again Slocum shrugged. "Reckon you could say that." You could say a good many other things, too, but Slocum did not think he particularly wanted to go into *those* occupational designations with a stranger.

"Lordy, oh, Lordy, a genu-wine cowboy. You ever shot anybody? Ever had you a gunfight?"

Slocum cocked an eyebrow and peered down at the obviously adoring youngster standing beside his boot.

"Right curious, aren't you. Well I'll tell you one thing, son, even if it ain't exactly what you asked me to say. Where I come from there's things a man don't ask. You've managed to find a few of 'em right there."

The boy looked as thrilled as if Slocum had just admitted to being Wild Bill Hickok or John Wesley Hardin.

Slocum stepped down off the right side of the horse, calming now, to stand beside Boyd. The kid began to look upset.

"I thought all cowboys only got on or off the left side of the horse."

Slocum laughed. "You ever do any riding in the high country, boy? Crossed any mountain ranges?" He looked around at the griddle-cake flatland that surrounded them here and answered his own question with a shake of his darkly handsome head. "No, I reckon maybe you haven't. If you ever do, you'll find out quick enough, boy, that you get off on the *uphill* side. It don't matter worth a damn what side that is, 'less you're built like a clown on stilts. You jus' do whatever's convenient. Rules like that are for greenhorns."

Boyd looked positively thrilled. "Do you—"

Slocum cut him off. "Before you get too carried away here, son, there was some mention a little bit ago about a twenty-dollar gold piece. Which is the reason I put on that little Texas-style exhibition for you."

"Yes sir, yessir." The kid dug into his pocket and slapped the shiny coin into Slocum's palm. "Cripes, I bet you'd shoot me plumb daid if I tried to welsh on you, wouldn't you, mistuh?"

Slocum looked at him with amusement glinting in his eyes. "Something like that," he agreed.

"Jesus."

"Well look, this has been kinda fun an' all that, but I got to get going. Gotta find my way back to Texas somehow, and I don't think twenty dollars is going to be enough to buy passage." Slocum nodded to the boy and would have turned away, but the kid grabbed at his shirt-sleeve.

Slocum looked down at the offending hand. "That ain't real bright, boy. Could be unhealthy."

"Oh." Boyd let go of the cloth like it had caught on fire. "I'm sorry. Honest. But lookaheah. If you're lookin' for work, why, my daddy 'n' me run the best spread between Okeechobee an' the St. Mary's Rivuh, an' that's a fact. We could give you a job. Top pay, too. Whatever they're payin' top hands out west, mistuh. Whatever that is."

"That's a hundred a month, boy," Slocum lied. Hell, the kid didn't know any better.

"That's it then, mistuh. A hundred a month. That's what I'm offerin' you. Firm."

Slocum rubbed his jaw, pretending to think it over. Actually it only reminded him that he needed a shave. Among other things. A hundred a month was a good wage. And there seemed little point in putting a string of wanted posters behind him in this part of the country. Not that he expected ever to come back, but he had heard that the law in this populated end of the country cheated a man by using the telegraph and cooperative extraditions to bother men who otherwise might have gone quietly about their business in the states and counties where there was no paper hung on them.

No, he thought, at a hundred a month he could afford to play it safe.

"Reckon I could take you up on that," he drawled.

The only problem was, John Slocum was not playing things nearly as safe as he thought he was.

12

Best place between Someplace and Whatchamacallit, huh? Slocum thought skeptically. It damn sure didn't look like the best of anything, except maybe heat and bugs and dripping sweat. Under other, better circumstances Slocum would have *paid* a hundred a month to stay out of a miserable country like this. Unfortunately, he just didn't have that option. He would simply have to grin and bear it until he could get the hell out of here.

All the way from that unnamed crossroads to the big, shabby house under a spread of oak and magnolia limbs, Boyd had been a chatterbox of excited questions, grilling Slocum about any and everything he might remember about the big-grass country west of the Mississippi.

Now, in the shadow of his home, the boy became withdrawn and apparently shy. Slocum wondered if the kid was having second thoughts about dragging home a stranger with the promise of a high-paying job. Judging from the appearances of the cowboys they were riding with, a hundred dollars must be closer to an annual wage here than a monthly one.

Slocum gave a mental shrug to the question of whether Boyd's offer would hold up once it was brought to the attention of the he-coon of the outfit. Even if the old man decided to tell the kid hell no, Slocum thought, they would at least feed him before they turned him back out onto the road. And he did have that double eagle in his pocket. The day was already showing a clear profit, and a man can't ask for much more than that in an always uncertain life.

"The folks'll be proud to meet yuh, John," Boyd said as they neared the house.

"Right." Slocum kept his doubts to himself.

Boyd and Slocum drew rein at the front of the house while the cowboys went on around back, driving the prize bull ahead of them, one of them trailing behind with the empty freight wagon.

The house itself was not exactly what Slocum would have pictured as the grand manor of the neighborhood. It was basically an over-large clapboard shack that had been added onto and added onto again so many times that now it sprawled, a collection of single-story shacks and verandas connected into an ungainly whole, not a board of which had ever seen a coat of paint. Moreover, most of the boards seemed to be warped and sagging. Slocum had seen mining-camp cribs that were built better and presented a better appearance than this.

"What d'yuh think?" Boyd asked proudly.

"Big ol' place, ain't it," Slocum said. That part at least was no lie. As he had hoped, Boyd accepted the statement as a compliment.

The two stepped down out of their saddles, Slocum still riding the horse he had borrowed from Boyd and the kid mounted on an animal that one of the cowboys had been riding until he was told to end the journey in the freight wagon—and hadn't Slocum gotten a dirty look about that order.

As soon as their feet hit the ground there was a movement in the deep shadows of the nearest veranda overhang, and a scrawny Negro dressed in rags came hurrying out to take the horses away. The little black man had gray tinging his wooly hair and was quite certainly a former slave.

Convenient, Slocum thought. A dollar a month pay on the books to make things legal, and down here in the swamplands slavery could go right on. Slocum had seen stray dogs that looked better cared for than this old man. Not that it was John Slocum's problem. All he wanted around here was to get gone from it.

"This way, John."

Slocum followed Boyd across the veranda and through

the door. Inside it was darker but not much cooler than it had been outside.

They passed through a hallway with a bare floor and bare walls into a large room filled with overstuffed furniture, some rag rugs on the floor, and a small table with some sort of board game set up on it. There was no fireplace, nor any provision for heat that Slocum could see.

"Pa, Mama, I got someone here I want you should meet."

Warren and Julia Calder stood for the introductions that Boyd performed. Both were impeccably dressed, clothed as a gentleman and his lady despite their surroundings. The tone of elegant respectability stopped there, though.

Warren Calder was every bit as tall as Slocum, but where Slocum was a tower of solid, ropy muscle, Calder was near to skinny. He had thinning black hair plastered flat against his head and a pencil-line mustache that emphasized the pallor of his skin. His eyes were dark and set rather too close together, and his undershot chin gave an impression not so much of weakness as . . . Slocum thought about it for a moment while he was smiling and shaking and nodding politely. The man reminded him of a weasel. Perhaps one of those black-footed ferrets you found up in Wyoming, except not nearly so sleek and handsome as a ferret. Slocum mumbled the polite noises that were expected of him and turned to greet the mother.

Julia Calder was a large woman, nearly as tall as her husband but much heavier. She had a bosom that could have rivaled the prow of the old *Amalie*, and she was built in proportion to it. A large woman tending now toward fat, she looked like she might have been more than a handful a score or so of years before. She was not pretty, and she was not a lady: In spite of her clothing, her carriage and a certain hardness in her features gave her away on that score. But she did look like she might have been a wild ride once upon a time.

Again Slocum made the appropriate sounds and complimentary remarks that were expected of a guest. He accepted the hand that she offered and bowed low over it, making a leg dutifully. It had been years since he had done that. And then he had been wearing gray and there had been a sword dangling at his side. The gesture brought back a flood of memory, of a time when good and bad had seemed so well defined and the future had stretched out in glorious anticipation. It made Slocum feel old and perhaps a bit sad to remember that now.

"Ma'am," he said politely, barely touching the tips of her fingers with his own hard hand.

"My my, what *do* we have here? A gentleman? La, I never thought to see the like, not in Calder Hall."

The voice came not from Julia Calder but from off to the side. Slocum rose from his bow and turned to look.

"That's my crazy sister," Boyd said. "Don't pay her no mind."

Pay her no mind? A brass statue wouldn't be able to avoid noticing her, Slocum thought. Shee-it.

Rose Calder was . . . extraordinary. Slocum was barely able to restrain himself. He wanted to gape. He very nearly did.

As tall as her mother, and taller than Boyd, she had a chest every bit as large as her mother's but with no trace of the fat that surrounded Julia's impressive mammaries. She was tall and full-bodied but had a waist that nipped down to tiny proportions and a swell of hip beneath that made Slocum's crotch warm.

Honey-colored hair was pinned into a mass of curls and curlicues around a delicately formed face. Rich, red, full lips. Straight nose. Warren Calder's dark eyes. High cheekbones. She had gotten her body from her mother and her face from her father, but the features that on Warren Calder looked pinched and weasel-like on Rose were delicate and refined.

A woman who had that much impact fully dressed would be damn near unbearable naked, Slocum thought.

Enough to give a man heart failure before he could ever get the bedspread thrown back. Damn, he thought.

He was already hoping the father would honor Boyd's job offer. Slocum definitely wanted to stay here a little while longer. Definitely.

He managed to hide the drooling lechery he was feeling, though, and turned with feigned disinterest to accept the introductions Boyd performed once again.

"Honored," Slocum said.

Again he made a leg and bowed low over the offered hand, but this time he did not quite touch the extended fingertips but only bowed over them.

If he had touched her he might well have made a grab for her, right there in the Calder living room with her mother and father watching.

Besides, a woman like this one—she could have been a year either side of Boyd's age, certainly old enough to be called a woman—would have every man she met drooling over her. As Slocum was himself inside. A little show of pretended disinterest at this point just might go a long way come nightfall.

Rose was obviously surprised that he did not take her offered hand, and before she had a chance to recover from that surprise, Slocum had straightened and turned away from her.

"You said something about showing me your setup here," he reminded Boyd. "How about it?"

"Don't go so far that you can't heah the dinner bell," Boyd's mother said.

Slocum's back was to Rose, but he would have sworn that he could feel heat radiating from her lush body. He hustled Boyd the hell out of there before a tent-pole protrusion at his fly could betray what he was really thinking about.

He wanted to tear off several large, juicy chunks of Boyd Calder's sister. His intention was to do exactly that.

13

The tap on the door was light, as if whoever was doing it did not want to be heard beyond the small, hot room Slocum had been given for the night. It was not, he thought, the sort of knock Boyd might give. Besides, Boyd had gone to bed a half hour or so ago.

"Come in, Boyd," Slocum said with a grin. He turned his back on the door and continued to give himself a sponge bath out of a bowl of tepid water. The heat and the humidity were stifling, and he felt sour with undried sweat. The water, warm as it was, felt good.

He heard the door open and turned around, straightening. He was naked, knots of solid muscle standing out up and down the long, lean length of him.

The visitor was, as Slocum had more than half suspected, Rose Calder.

Slocum stood looking into her eyes, tall and darkly handsome and very well aware of it. "I thought it was Boyd," he lied. He made no effort to cover himself.

Rose stood with the door open, half into his room, her gaze drawn inevitably to the massive tool that hung between Slocum's powerful thighs. Involuntarily her tongue tip darted out and licked at her own full lips. "I . . . wanted to tell you good night."

"Bullshit," Slocum said.

The girl's eyes flicked away from Slocum's groin for an instant, then returned. "I . . ."

"Shut the door," he ordered. She did as she was told.

Slocum dropped the washcloth he had been using into the basin and took his time about toweling himself dry.

When he was done he took the few strides necessary to cross the small room and stand before the tall, lovely young woman. She had not moved during that time except to follow his every motion with her eyes.

Now her eyes met Slocum's, then closed as he reached out and began to undo the long line of tiny buttons that held her dress closed from throat to waist.

Slocum parted the cloth and slipped the garment from her shoulders. Again there was that telltale flicker of tongue to lips. Slocum grinned.

Nude, she was as beautiful as he had imagined she would be. Her body was exquisite, a Grecian statue in flesh and bone. He picked her up—she was a big woman, and a lesser man couldn't have managed it—and carried her to the bed.

He placed her on the bed and sat beside her, allowing his hands to run lightly across the warm, silken hollows and curves of her. Her eyes remained closed, but pearl-white teeth nibbled at her underlip and she began to moan softly as he touched her.

"You didn't come to say good night," Slocum said.

"No," she agreed. She parted her legs to his probing touch. "I didn't."

"Why did you come then?"

"You know."

"Tell me."

"Must I?"

"Tell me."

She moaned with the pleasure his fingers were giving her. She shifted her hips on the yielding bed and opened herself more fully to him. "You already know."

"Tell me," he insisted.

Her eyes came open, and she drank in the sight of him, from his dark, hard-chiseled face, down the flat planes of his chest to the throbbing, steel-hard erection that pulsed red with engorged blood at his groin. She licked her lips again. "For that," she whispered.

"What?"

"For that." She seemed unable to look away from it.

Her voice stronger now, she said, "I came because I want that. I want you to fuck me, John Slocum."

Slocum grinned. "Make me."

It was a challenge.

"I can, you know."

"Prove it."

"Yes."

The girl rolled onto her side and took her eyes from Slocum's cock long enough to grin back at him. The challenge was understood and accepted.

She reached up and drew him down onto the bed beside her, then gathered herself and came to her knees over him. "Roll over," she instructed.

Slocum's eyebrows went up in wonder. It was an odd request. But he did what she asked.

He was glad that he had.

He felt the warmth of her breath first, then the first light nip of her lips, finally the slow, languid touch of her moving tongue.

She started at the nape of his neck, and Slocum was surprised and pleased to learn how sensitive he was to her touch there.

She knew what she was doing, and she took her time about it. She began on the back of his neck and continued around to the extremely sensitive tissues behind his ears, then down onto his powerful shoulders and upper back.

There was not a square inch of flesh that she did not touch and savor with her lips and her tongue.

She braced herself over him with her arms so that the only contact between them was at her mouth. Even her hair, pinned up as it was, did not reach him. Only that hot, wet, moving mouth.

She moved lower, exploring his back and buttocks. She pressed lightly with her fingertips to get him to move his legs apart, and her honeyed tongue slid between the cheeks of his ass to lick and probe and tantalize Slocum's anus and scrotum. He had been ready before;

now he thought he might very well explode in a massive spray of boiling cum.

Rose moved lower, tasting of his thighs and calves. She lingered for some time at the backs of his knees—also more sensitive than he would have believed—and took her time about sucking on each toe, exploring with her tongue each socket between his toes.

"Roll over again," she ordered. This time there was no hesitation about doing as she asked.

She worked her way slowly back up his legs, skipped his midsection and began again at his head, licking and tasting and teasing his closed eyes, his nose and ears, down to his throat and across his chest and belly.

Finally, when Slocum thought he could take no more, she reached the object of her long search and drew him deep into her mouth.

Slocum groaned. He did not want to, but he was unable to prevent it. The wait had been so long. And so fine.

Her mouth bathed him in heat, and Slocum lay back and let the sensations flood through him. She drew him in deep and then pulled back away from him, pulling against the strong suction she was applying.

He burst free from her with a soft, moist plop of wet sound, and unexpectedly she laughed. She sounded pleased with herself.

She had every right to feel pleased with herself, Slocum decided.

He did not know if he had ever been so hard, so ready.

She licked his balls, ran her darting tongue up the enormous shaft of him, took him deep into her mouth again. Again there was that moist, delightful sound when he burst free from the warm confinement.

"There," she said. "Have I proved it?"

Slocum wanted to grab her and throw her onto her back, to fling her legs apart and spear her until she screamed. Perversely, though, he refused to give her that satisfaction. Not yet.

"I can wait," he said.

Rose looked shocked. She seemed not to know what to do next nor how to go about it.

Slocum laughed. He sat up and reached out to cup one large, pink-tipped breast in his hand.

He squeezed. Hard. He knew it hurt her, but it seemed to give her more pleasure than it gave her pain. She closed her eyes, and her mouth—hot, inviting, talented—sagged open. She moaned. She was limp under his demanding touch.

Slocum released her breast and moved his hard, powerful hand to the back of her neck.

He pushed her head roughly down onto him, forcing himself into her to a depth greater than she had been able to accept before. She made no effort to struggle, and when she tried to swallow, the throbbing head of his massive cock slipped past the constriction of her throat, and he was all the way inside her.

"Now," he said, "that's good enough."

He pulled her away from him and took her by the shoulders.

He pressed her back onto the bed, and there was no need for him to spread her legs. They were already apart, and the tight curls of her pubic hair were wet with droplets of her anticipation of him inside her.

Slocum knelt between her thighs and kneaded both breasts with his large, strong hands. She bit her lip and seemed to be having difficulty trying not to cry out aloud.

"Ask for it," he ordered her roughly.

"Yes," she said. "Please. *Please*."

With a wolflike grin of satisfaction, John Slocum poised his huge tool at the parted lips of her waiting sex. He paused there, each throb of his heartbeat pulsing insistently against her, until her eyes opened pleadingly, and once again she whispered, "Please."

With a short bark of laughter, Slocum flung himself forward.

14

Slocum was ready when the Negro maid called him to breakfast, but it was only his strong constitution and a long-standing habit of early rising that permitted this. The night had been a long one and he still felt drained by it.

The Calder family had already gathered in the dining room, with the exception of Rose, who seemed to be sleeping in late this morning. Somehow Slocum did not find that to be particularly surprising.

"Mornin'," Slocum said.

The answers, and the expressions worn by Boyd and his parents, told Slocum that all the whinnying and grunting in his bedroom had gone unnoticed by the rest of the family.

He sat, and another servant offered him platters of fried pork and bowls of gravy and grits. It had been years since Slocum had tasted grits. He had come to despise the weavil-infested slop that passed for grits during the war years. He discovered that time and an improved, civilian version of the stuff had not led to any changes in his opinion on that subject.

"You'll be ready to start work today?" the elder male Calder asked when Slocum was half done with his meal.

"Whenever you want me to," Slocum said.

Table conversation in Calder Hall, as the girl had referred to the place the evening before, was to the point and seldom, it seemed. The Calders took their eating seriously.

"Today," Boyd's father grunted. He reached for the platter of pork, appeared not to find a piece that was to his liking, and glared over his shoulder at the harried-looking serving girl. She almost fell in her rush to reach Warren Calder's side and supply his desires.

Slocum wondered once again what had become of the myth that slavery was no more. It sure seemed to be in fashion around Calder Hall.

Nice folks, Slocum thought.

John Slocum had worn butternut and gray during the war. He had given it the best that was in him to give. But he had fought for a nation, not for the institution of slavery. And since that time he had known men both good and bad whose skins were glossy black. He had fought against some and alongside others, and he had come to the conclusion that you just can't tell a whole hell of a lot about a man from the way he looks. He doubted that Warren Calder held that same opinion, though. The man acted like he believed his shit didn't stink.

Still, Warren Calder was willing to pay Slocum a hundred dollars a month to work cattle—or maybe it was to amuse Boyd and spin lies to the kid about the Wild-fucking-West—so he was entitled to hold any opinions he damn well pleased. John Slocum would happily accept his pay and bide his time, and just as quickly as he possibly could he would head for Texas and some people and surroundings that he understood and could be comfortable in.

There was just no damned way a man could be comfortable in this miserable country. You woke up sweating, you went to bed sweating, and it was damn near too hot and muggy for a man to want to bump bellies with a woman. Damn near, but not quite.

Slocum sighed. The sooner he got back to some high, dry country the better.

He glanced into the corner where a pair of monster-sized roaches—palmetto bugs, Boyd had called them—were amusing themselves, and he scowled. No one else seemed to be paying any attention at all to the roaches. That was what Slocum really disliked about it. The little bastards were so common here that they were not remarkable enough to stomp on. This was indeed a shitty piece of country, Slocum thought.

"You all done, John?"

"Ready anytime you are, Boyd."

They left the table, and Slocum followed the kid out into the brassy glare of a newly risen sun. The day was going to be a sonuvabitch for hot.

The regular cowboys apparently ate elsewhere, because they were already assembled at the corrals, mounted on their skinny bangtails and sitting single-fire saddles that looked like a cross between the open-seat McClellan and some bastard version of a Mexican rig. None of them looked to be overjoyed by Slocum's presence. Which was hardly amazing, Slocum reflected. The poor clods probably didn't make fifteen dollars a month, and they would have overheard Boyd's offer the day before.

That was not, Slocum realized, an offer calculated to endear him to the other hands on the place.

Not that Slocum really gave a shit. He wanted to grab and go just as quickly as possible, and he felt no particular compulsion to be buddy-buddy with those around him. Slocum was a loner at the best of times. And being here was not something he would consider to be the very best of times. They were welcome to hate his bloody guts, each and every one of them, just so long as they didn't interfere with him getting back to Brownsville.

"Pay attention now, boys," the kid informed them. "We got us a *real* cowboy from the western country here, an' he's gonna show us how they do it in Texas, he is. So mount up"—they already *were* mounted—"an' we'll git on with it."

The boy was well-meaning, Slocum decided, but stupid as a boar hog in heat.

Oh well, he had a sister wild enough to make up for the kid's various shortcomings.

Slocum tightened his cinch—it had been hanging loose even though the horse was handed over to him supposedly ready to ride—and checked to make sure some joker had not cut his reins at the bits or something humorous like that. Then he cheeked the horse with its muzzle back against the stirrup—he knew damn good and well it would be the rankest animal they had on the place—and prepared himself for a storm when he got into the saddle.

There had to be easier ways than this to earn a dollar, he thought. It was just that, around here, he didn't know any. Pity.

15

"How did I know it'd be you that was knock-knock-knockin' at my door?" Slocum grinned and stepped back. Rose closed the door behind her.

"Surely you aren't going to pretend that you don't want me, dear John." She was wearing a wraparound robe of some flimsy material. She unbelted it and let it fall from her shoulders, standing gloriously naked before him. She was statuesque in perhaps the truest sense of that word. Big and beautiful and lusciously shaped. Slocum felt himself beginning to rise to the offer.

He believed, though, that this gorgeous—and insatiable—woman was not one he could ever let know how she affected him. If she ever knew, he was sure, she could be a prick-teasing bitch of the first water. There was enough of the arrogance of her father, and enough self-awareness of her own beauty and desirability, to guarantee that, he felt.

So he kept his face a blank and turned away from her. "It's been a long, hot day. I'm filthy dirty and covered with sweat. And I'm tired. Of course you're always welcome to sit down and finger yourself. I won't bother you."

Rose quite obviously did not know how to take him. Which was just exactly what Slocum wanted. She hurried around to place herself in front of him and molded her naked body to his smelly one.

"I don't care about that. Really I don't, John. Make love to me tonight. Please."

"Make love?" He laughed. "Lust, sure. But I wouldn't call it love, darlin'."

"All right. Fuck me, then. Please."

He shrugged. Hell, it was one thing to be hard to get. He damned sure didn't want to make it impossible. "I need a bath," he said.

Rose brightened. "I'll give you a bath, then. I'd do that for you. I'd . . . do *any*thing for you."

"A bath like last night's?"

"If that's what you want, John."

"We'll see, then. A sponge bath first." He shucked out of his sweaty clothing, wishing he had a change of clothes he could put on in the morning rather than crawling yet again into these foul garments, and lay down on the bed. The sheets still smelled faintly of the workout he and Rose had already given them.

Rose poured water from the pitcher, apparently refilled by a servant some time during the day, and sopped the washcloth first in the basin and then in a jar of soft, homemade soap. She bent over Slocum, seemingly unmindful of her nakedness for the moment, and began to bathe him.

It was pleasant, he admitted to himself, but still he willed himself to remain limp under her touch.

If he had gone panting and lusting after her ass, he was sure, Boyd's baby sister Rose would have laughed in his face and slapped him down.

But ignore a beautiful woman and she will take it as a challenge. And bust her butt if that was what it would take to arouse some interest.

Rose washed him and dried him, lingering longest at Slocum's crotch and giving him a taste test for any remaining traces of salty sweat.

Finally she pronounced him clean.

By then, of course, Slocum had long since lost his battle to stay limp and loose. There was no concealing from her now the fact that he was more than ready for what she had in mind.

"Would you like another tongue bath?" she asked.

"No," Slocum told her curtly.

The girl smiled. "I was hoping you'd say that. I'm so hot an' ready, honey, that I think I'll bust if you don't get it in me soon.'' She snuggled down onto the bed beside him and wrapped her arms around him, trying to wriggle ever closer and to kiss him.

Slocum drew his face away from hers. "Roll over.''

"What?''

"Belly down on the bed, woman.''

"But what . . . ?''

"You've heard of a piece of ass?''

"I've heard the expression, yes, but . . .''

"So roll over.''

Rose's eyes widened. She looked frightened. "I've never done it that way before. And you're so *huge*.''

"Roll over,'' Slocum repeated.

She did as she was told, glancing back over her smooth-skinned shoulder with the fear plain in her large, dark eyes.

This was all right, Slocum thought. The woman would do any damn thing he asked now. Anything.

He knelt between her legs and fingered her. She was already wet from her anticipation, and he probed deep inside her, making her quiver and moan in spite of her fear of his size and intended entry.

Slocum wet his fingers thoroughly with the woman-juices she had to spare and then, more gently than she must have expected, caressed the pink and brown rose-bud that lay between the cheeks of her round, lovely ass.

He probed inside her there, slowly at first, then more vigorously.

"Oh . . . that . . . it feels good there. I didn't know . . .''

Slocum withdrew his hand and dropped a dollop of spit onto his fingertips to add to the juices she had provided. She was moist and ready to accept him now, and he guided himself into her.

The trick, he knew, was not to go too fast. If he plunged into her now she would tighten up, and the pain would be excruciating. That was a mistake he was not likely to make.

He entered her slowly, a fraction of an inch at a time, and he could feel her relax and accept him as more and more of his incredible length sank out of sight into the depths of the girl's ass.

She was as tight there as a grade-school virgin, and she was clamped around him like one of those gum-rubber devices weaker men sometimes used to strengthen their flagging erections. Slocum grinned as he felt himself reach full depth within Rose's body. Damn, but this one had a body a man could walk a mile on.

Slowly, still giving her time to relax and learn to accept him, he began to pump gently in and out, withdrawing more of himself with each renewed stroke and gradually driving back into her with more and more power.

Rose began to moan with her own pleasure and started to hump her ass back into him, meeting him stroke for stroke now, herself stepping up the pace, her body begging for more and stronger penetration.

She was panting in time with her efforts, and, incredibly, he could feel the thin, quavering dance of deep-muscle spasms that told him she was rising toward a climax too.

He gave up the caution he had been displaying until then and allowed himself to plunge and surge deeper and harder, reaching around to clutch at her tits while he rode her like a bucking mare, pumping and driving and abandoning himself wholly. At that moment he didn't care if he split her in two; he only wanted to burst forth as deeply inside her as he could reach.

The explosion began deep in his balls, and he could feel the white-hot flow of cum rush out of his scrotum and up the shaft of his cock until it sprayed forth like a burst of molten lead.

Rose shrieked into Slocum's pillow as he came, and he could feel the buck and leap of her own climax as she came with him.

Slocum collapsed on top of her back, this time not caring about the sticky sweat that glued his flesh to hers.

Both of them were breathing in short, strained gasps. "That," he said, "was just for starters."

16

It was interesting and all that, but, damn, it was tiring trying to keep up with virtually two jobs at once. The first, of course, was what he had been hired to do, which was to handle cattle on the sprawling, swampy land that was the Calder ranch.

The other job was trying to keep up with the insatiable and still growing demands of Rose Calder.

Not that Slocum *minded*. Exactly. But a man has to have some time to sleep, too.

And if his night job was frequently exhausting, his day job, with the cattle, was even more frequently confusing.

It seemed that these tropical cowboys had a different way of doing damn near everything there was to be done with a cow or a calf.

There was not a hand among them who could be sure of hitting the ground with a rope if he dropped the damn thing. Yet any among them could make a fifteen-foot length of bullhide whip stand up and talk in a manner that even an out-west bullwhacker could not match. Those boys could pluck posies with the crackers on their whips, Slocum was convinced.

And they regarded the term "cracker" itself as a high honor among their kind, which was another revelation.

Back during his soldiering days, John Slocum had served with more than a few old boys from Georgia and Alabama, and he had come to understand—from one group and about the other—that a good ol' boy being called a cracker was being called poor white trash. It was an insult deep enough to be regarded as deadly under some circumstances.

Down here to call a man a cracker was to pay him a compliment.

A Georgia cracker was a man so poor or so lazy that he didn't have a crop or the means to provide himself with a meal, so he cracked open tidal shellfish to eke out a miserable meal.

A Florida cracker was a cowman or a cowboy who had a long and agile cracker on the end of his whip and who considered himself the equal of any and the better of most. The difference was startling.

And *every*thing about a Florida cracker was damn well different from the cowhands Slocum had known in all his previous experience.

The saddles they rode were small, lightweight, actually quite flimsy things in comparison with their western counterparts. The western cowhand needed the strength of sheer mass when he tied a rope to his saddle horn and used it to drag down a fighting longhorn, while the southern cracker handled his animals with whips and dogs and corral chutes, often enough working on foot in or on a chute where a westerner would have used ropes and horsepower out in the open to get the same jobs done.

The horses those flimsy saddles were placed on would have seemed undernourished scrubs compared with western cow ponies, including the small but agile and sturdy mustang strains. The Florida horses were . . . atrocious, Slocum thought. Undersized, poorly formed, awkward of foot, and constantly afflicted with diseases, worms, rotting hoofs, and seemingly a thousand other ailments.

Much like the cattle they were used to herd.

Slocum decided quickly that he had never before seen such an ailing group of livestock as these southern cattle.

Ticks and screwworms and rotting hoofs from unceasing exposure to moisture were only the most visible of their problems. They were also just plain malnourished.

Slocum would have thought that stock would stay fat

and sassy in a country where the grass never browned
and the trees never lost their green. That would only
stand to reason, he thought.

He would have been damn well wrong. And was.

Instead it turned out that the soft sand that was the
soil of this hot, humid country held no food value at all.
The grass it grew in such abundance seemed to be just
so much green pulp that would fill a cow's belly without giving it much in the way of benefit. Horse and cow
alike could graze day and night and still remain on the
brink of starvation with their bellies stuffed full.

And the deer they passed as they rode through the
wetland pastures. Slocum had not been able to stifle a
bark of incredulous laughter the first time he saw a
Florida whitetail deer.

Used to the magnificence of the high-country mule
deer and the fluid grace of the plains whitetail, Slocum
had almost failed to recognize these distant cousins as
being deer at all.

The poor creatures were about the same size as a
decently fed redbone hound. Smaller, actually, than
most guard dogs. Slocum had gone so far as to rein in
the hammerheaded, potbellied horse he was riding that
day and ask if he had seen correctly.

"Damn straight," the answer had been. "Good deah
aroun' heah. Ol' Jimmy ovuh theah, he got him one
helluva buck outta that hummock a while back. That
buck dressed over sixty pound, I'm tellin' yuh."

Slocum believed it. At that rate a carcass would give
each man in the crew little more than a mouthful of
meat. He shook his head in mingled disgust and wonder
and rode on.

Actually, he realized, if these crackers' ways were
strange to him, his methods must have seemed equally
outlandish to them.

And it helped matters not at all that Boyd Calder's
growing hero-worship of everything western and everything Slocum was so obvious to the crackers.

None of the crackers was so impolite as to say anything directly to him about it, but Slocum could feel their resentment growing as the days and the work went on.

At the nooning fires Slocum took his meals with Boyd or, if the boy was not along on that day's ride, alone. There was no camaraderie between the crackers and himself, no bridge of common experience. He rode and he worked beside them but not really with them.

Not that Slocum gave a shit. Or so he told himself. He was only there long enough to earn his passage back across the Gulf to Brownsville. These were not friends he was riding with, and they were not likely to become friends. They were just . . . there. And he would stick it out for as long as he had to. Not a moment longer.

So he rode and he marveled and he marked the passage of time as another few paces closer to the opportunities that were waiting for him in Mexico on that volatile border.

And there were always the nights for him to find comfort in.

17

"Yes. Please. Now. Now!" Rose's lush body was slippery with sweat. She lay beneath him, panting rapidly, her hips rotating and pumping beyond control, rising to meet him, demanding to be entered. "Please, John."

Slocum's lips drew back in a grin. He taunted her yet again, dipping only the red, engorged head of his cock between the lips of her sex and then quickly withdrawing before she could raise herself to him and take him inside herself. This was a woman who was used to having her own way, but she had soon enough learned that this was a man who was her master.

"Please. Don't make me wait . . . aah-h-h-h-h!!!"

Slocum rammed himself hip-deep into the yielding softness of her eager body, and she clamped herself to him with a fiercely joyous strength.

He held himself rigid above her and let her own frantic thrashing carry her to and beyond the brink of pleasure. At the last instant Rose bit into the slabs of hard muscle on Slocum's shoulder to stifle the screams that would have told the rest of the household about her release. She bucked and shuddered beneath him and fell back sobbing onto the sweat-soaked sheets.

With an iron control, Slocum refused to allow himself to give in to the orgasm she was desperately trying to wring from him. Not yet, he told himself. Not so easy as all that.

Slocum withdrew from her, the length of him dripping with the juices of her desires, and rolled onto his back beside her. Her fingers crept softly down to his crotch and encircled him. "You didn't make it."

"I will," he assured her. "When I'm ready."

She looked at him with heavy-lidded eyes and made a pout with lips that were already puffy with love bruises. "What if I tell you you've worn me out, western man? What if I send you away now that you've given me what I wanted?"

Slocum laughed softly. "You won't."

She gave him a self-satisfied smile. "You don' think so, Johnny?"

"You can't," Slocum added softly.

This time she saw the wolfish grin that played without a hint of mirth on his lips. Her eyes widened and she seemed to realize that for the first time she had encountered a man she dared not taunt or tease.

"My family—" she began.

"—would die as quick as anybody else if they tried to fuck with me," Slocum finished for her. He rolled half on top of her, crushing her breasts against the hard planes of his chest. "But that won't happen," he said, "because nobody's going to know what me an' you like to do behind that locked door. 'Cause I sure ain't gonna holler, and I know you don't wanta quit neither."

He reached down and began to knead and probe the wet, tender flesh high in the vee of her crotch.

Rose's head lolled against the pillow and her eyes regained that sleepy, distant, heavy-lidded look they had so recently had. The pink tip of her tongue darted out to moisten bowed lips, and once again her hips took up the slow, timeless motion that his touch demanded of her body. Slocum did not need any more answer than that.

He touched and probed and tantalized with his fingers as her hips moved more and more rapidly in response to him, and Rose's breath came quicker and shorter.

After little more than seconds her breath caught in her throat. She arched her back and began to shudder lightly.

"Didn't reckon you'd mind," Slocum said drily.

He rolled onto his back again and stretched out beside her, looking up toward the mosquito netting that framed the huge, canopied bed in Rose's bedroom. He reached out with one powerful hand to find and to cup the back of her elegantly molded head. He began to urge her lovely face down toward his still throbbing cock.

"Can't I wait till I get my breath back an' . . ."

Slocum ignored her.

"Whatever you say, John," she said submissively.

The girl nuzzled into the heat of John Slocum's loins, and he allowed his legs to fall apart to receive her there.

His tool was still slimy with the wetness from having so recently been inside her. She bent to the task he had given her, though, and used the darting pink tip of her tongue to clean the woman-juices from him. Then she bent lower and slathered his cum-heavy balls with that same probing tongue, sending him higher and ever higher.

Slocum's head lolled back on the damp pillow and tossed from side to side as her quick-moving tongue probed and licked and caressed the sensitive flesh beneath the engorged sack of his balls. His lips drew back from his teeth in a grimace of intense pleasure.

"Now," he ordered. "All of it."

Rose shifted her position to comply. He could feel the teasing, feathery drag of soft hair across his scrotum, and she used delicately applied fingertips to continue the sensations on his balls while her attention moved upward.

The tip of her tongue flickered lightly at the small opening in the swollen red head of his throbbing penis. After a moment she cupped the length of him with her free hand and drew him closer to that lovely face now hidden by falling wings of velvet hair.

She wrapped her lips around him and moaned softly as she drew him into the warm cavity of her mouth.

Briefly she applied hard suction and pulled away, taking only the bulbous, glass-smooth head inside and then repeating the action, building and teasing until Slocum's hips began to gyrate in spite of himself and he shoved upward, trying to cram more and more of his awesome length into her.

His cock was slick with her saliva now, and Rose paused for a moment to turn and look at him with a triumphant smile of satisfaction. He wanted her desperately now, and she knew it.

Finally, she bent to him again, and this time she opened her jaws wide and pressed down against him.

Slocum could feel the head of his cock slip beyond the sweet wetness of her mouth to the constriction at her throat.

He could feel the instinctive closure of the ring of muscle and cartilage there, but the girl continued her pressure, forcing her head down toward the hard planes of his belly, and after a moment he slipped past that momentary blockage and was deep inside her throat.

He felt her body buck momentarily as she fought back an involuntary gag reflex.

Her head began to rise and fall in the ages-old rhythm of superior sex, and Slocum closed his eyes. He gave himself over fully to the sensations that swept through him and—too soon, too long, he could not have said which—the final sensation gushed like molten steel out of his balls and through the exquisitely sensitive tubes that ran through his cock.

His cum sprewed into her throat with a volcano's explosion, and Slocum groaned out loud, unable to contain the sound.

He fell back onto the bed limp and satiated.

In a moment or two, he knew, he would take her again. But for now he was replete with satisfaction.

For now, he had nothing more to give and wanted nothing more to take.

He sighed and did not mind when she pulled away from him, sitting up and stopping to smile, using that delightful tongue to lick away a milk-white droplet from the corner of her mouth.

"It isn't love," she whispered, "but it'll do." She giggled softly and cuddled close against his side.

18

"What's this?" Slocum asked. The crew, including Slocum and Boyd, was assembled in the yard beside the house instead of heading as usual for the corral to saddle and begin the workday.

"We're going down to the southeast edge of our range," Boyd said, as if that explained anything. Perhaps it did to the others, but not to Slocum.

"Yeah, sure," Slocum said. He rubbed a hand over eyes that were red and stinging from lack of sleep. Jeez, he told himself, what a wit I'm turning into. Clever comebacks to any ol' line the kid throws out.

Still, whatever they were waiting around for, it was all right by him. Leaping into a saddle and spending the whole damn day riding through steamy heat and clouds of mosquitoes was something he was willing to postpone just as long as they liked.

The crew stood in the already muggy air of the early morning and spoke to each other in soft undertones that Slocum did not try to overhear. None of the bastards liked him anyway, and he felt just exactly as kindly disposed toward them. They stood and bit off hunks from their chews or puffed on their pipes, and he stood with Boyd trying to force the fog from his brain that was brought on by the need for much more rest than he was getting these days.

Old man Calder made an appearance on the veranda after some minutes had gone by, and the crew began to shuffle closer to the house. Calder was carrying one end of a flat, wooden chest, and a black servant was at the other end.

"What's this?" Slocum asked.

Boyd grinned. "The reason I like goin' down t' that end o' the place. Pa don't allow no short guns aroun' here close t' home, but he figures it's all right down there. Can you, uh, shoot like some o' them fellas I've read about in the books?" the kid added eagerly. Slocum managed to refrain from shaking his head sadly at the boy.

"Short guns, huh?" A few, very few, of the crew carried shotguns or rifles slung at their saddles, and most of those were cut-down military castoffs that would have approximately the same lethal effect in a gunfight as would a hearty fart. Mostly the men carried only whips and belt knives. Now it seemed they were to be issued something more interesting.

Calder set the chest on the edge of the covered porch and threw back the lid. The thing was filled with rusting but familiar shapes. Cap-and-ball revolvers, either Colts or some of the many copies that had been produced in quantity in the South back during the war. Percussion guns were long since outmoded, Slocum knew, but they were also as durable as a hammer. And some of them, he recalled, had just about the same effective range, too. He gave a mental shrug and stepped into the line that was forming to receive the guns. Any five-shot weapon would be more effective than the single-tube horse pistol he had been carrying behind his belt.

Boyd stepped around the group of his father's employees and dipped a hand into the box. "Here, John, this'n's a good'un." He tossed Slocum a slim-barreled revolver that turned out to be a genuine Colt article, a .36 Navy model and not some shoddy imitation.

Slocum caught the gun deftly by the scarred walnut grips, and his finger automatically found the brass trigger guard. He allowed the weight of the gun to spin it into his hand, and a brief smile flickered over his thin, sometimes cruel lips. He had forgotten just how *good* an old .36 Navy felt in the hand. Light and beautifully balanced and shaped to fall into that same natural point that all Colts seemed to offer.

"Shee-it," he said. "Now that's all right."

"Here's a holster for it." Boyd threw him a black leather pouch with its belt loop on the wrong side and no rake at all in the way it would hang. It was obviously a military surplus cavalry holster with its protective flap cut away. As a quick-draw holster it was about as useful as a burlap sack, although a rig like that would do the job of carrying the revolver from place to place. Including, Slocum thought, to the cemetery. He shook his head and tossed the butchered Army holster back into the chest.

"A waistband's better than that thing," he said.

"I think you're wrong, John. All the pictures I've seen from out west, why, them fellas all carry their guns in holsters."

"You do it your way, Boyd, an' I'll do 'er mine." Slocum turned away and would have headed for the horses, but a voice from the group of cowboys stopped him.

"I told you them Texans was just a bag o' shit."

Slocum stopped where he was. Slowly, very slowly, he turned around to face the men. He was getting just a little bit tired of the attitude of these cracker cowboys.

"If the man who said that has guts enough to say it to my face," he said, "which I doubt, I would be mighty pleased to snap assholes with him."

There was an uneasy stirring among the men, but one of them sifted out toward the front after only a moment's hesitation.

"I said it," he declared. "I meant it."

"Luther, ain't it?"

"Uh huh. Honus Luther. An' I'm at *least* as good a man as you are, John Slocum."

"As good? Or as fast? There can be a whopping big difference between them."

"As good *and* as fast," Luther responded.

Slocum grinned at him, and the grin was not pleasant to see. "How would you like to prove it, Honus Luther?"

"There's one real good way that I can think of," Luther said.

Slocum laughed. "Let's load 'em up, then." The revolvers had been emptied and cleaned for storage.

Boyd Calder looked as thrilled as a kid with a new top, but his father stepped quickly forward. "I don't want anyone on this crew shooting up anybody else that works here. Or neither one of you will go on working here. Is that clear?"

Slocum turned ice-cold green eyes toward the elder Calder and said, "I really don't give a shit. If that silly prick over there is fool enough to draw on me, I don't figure to stand an' watch him till he's done."

Luther had looked like he would be willing to turn away until Slocum spoke, but it was obvious that he did not like Slocum's choice of words. He began to get red in the face, and his neck swelled like a buck in rut.

"Let 'em fight, Pa. Damn."

There was a murmuring among the men that said that they too would like to see Luther and the visitor have it out. No doubt, Slocum thought, they wanted to see this western fellow get his balls blown off by a good ol' cracker boy. He could understand their point of view without particularly appreciating it.

The feelings of the men were not lost on Calder. He pursed his lips and gave it a moment's thought. "I'll tell you what," he said finally. "Those guns ain't loaded yet. Why don't you slip some caps onto them nipples an' the rest of us will judge whose noise comes the quickest."

The suggestion gained quick and eager approval from the cowboys, although from Slocum it received nothing but disgust. These were supposed to be grown men, yet they were willing to play at death as if it were a child's game. He felt nothing but contempt for the suggestion.

Yet there was more than enough pride in him to make him want to show these stringy crackers that they were playing in a league where they did not belong.

"Whatever," he grunted.

Boyd was quick to jump on the opportunity for a show. He grabbed a tin of percussion caps from the chest and rushed first to Slocum's side and then to Luther's.

It was stupid, Slocum thought. But damn-all he was tired of these ignorant crackers. He slipped the crimped brass percussion caps onto the nipples of the ancient Colt and jammed the long, octagonal barrel into his waistband.

Honus Luther was grinning happily now. He could put on his show and make his taunts without endangering a single drop of his own blood.

The man fitted the caps into place on his revolver and took his time about arranging his holster in exactly the correct spot on his belt. He stood, he crouched, he swung his arms back and forth, several times he pawed at the gun butt that was nearly buried in the leather dangling from his belt. Slocum stood back and watched him with a bored expression on his lean, dark face.

Once he glanced up toward the house. Boyd was looking positively enthralled with the whole thing. Slocum thought the kid might be about to have his first orgasm. Beyond him there was another and much prettier face showing in an open window. Rose was watching them too.

Slocum scowled. He had felt no necessity to show off for a pretty girl since he was old enough to get his first piece of ass. He did not particularly want to start that kind of juvenile behavior now, either.

On the other hand he did seem to be stuck with it, idiotic or not. He sighed and returned his attention to Honus Luther. The cracker seemed finally to be satisfied that he was good and ready for a cap-gun shoot-out.

Shee-it, Slocum thought. The man could have died a dozen times by now if any of this game was for real.

"Are you boys ready?" Calder asked.

"You damn well betcha," Luther said. Slocum just grunted. He had been ready for years.

"On the count of three . . ."

"Naw," Slocum said. "There ain't no point in that kind of shit. When a fight's for real you don't get to wind up an' get ready for it. Just let the man have at it whenever he wants. I'll be standing right here."

Luther grinned and so did most of the crackers. Slocum was giving Luther an edge. Or so they thought. They liked that idea just fine.

"You sure about that, Texan?" Luther growled. "Or do you just want an excuse?"

Slocum shrugged. "No excuses. But first you gotta be faster." He was standing upright and loose, seemingly paying no attention to his make-believe opponent. His eyes seemed to be drifting off toward the window where Rose was watching.

Luther, though, was wound up as tight as a two-bit watch. He began to crouch, and his fingers curled into a claw above the grips of his revolver.

Luther began to grin. He was going to positively enjoy humiliating this chickenshit strutter from Texas. You bet.

He took a deep breath, let out half of it, and tensed himself, ready to spring into action. A nerve ending at the corner of his mouth began to twitch. Anytime now he would be ready and . . .

His hand swept down toward the butt of his revolver.

John Slocum was standing relaxed and thoughtful, seemingly paying no attention. The cowboys, knowing it would be Luther's move first, were watching Honus Luther's hand.

And so practically none of them saw any motion at all from Slocum.

As far as they could tell, one instant Slocum was standing looking toward the girl inside the house and the very next instant that slim, deadly Colt had appeared in his fist and the gun was aimed directly at Honus Luther's belly.

By the time Luther's hand closed around the grips of his revolver they had heard at least two, some said three, loud pops as the caps from Slocum's Colt exploded. Before the barrel of Luther's revolver came level with the top of his holster, Slocum's .36 Navy was empty of its five caps.

"That fast!" someone breathed in the crowd of cowboys. "Why, nobody could be accurate that quick."

Slocum looked that way and grinned. "Let's try it again, then. But this time with bullets."

Whoever it was who had spoken did not identify himself. And several of the men turned their faces away.

Luther, Slocum noticed, was not saying anything. He stood with his gun half out of his holster, his face chalk-white from shock.

He had thought he was good, but . . .

"If you boys are done playing," Slocum suggested, "we might go out an' get some work done."

The cracker cowboys were very quiet now as they drifted away.

19

When Calder got around to issuing ammunition for the cap-and-ball revolvers he also issued blankets and food enough for several days. Slocum began to wonder just how big the Calder range was. He had always been under the impression that all of the South was chopped up into ten-acres-and-a-mule little pieces. Now it seemed it was his turn to be surprised about the difference between myth and reality.

As usual Boyd was in charge of the crew, and they rode for most of the day before setting up camp near a slow-moving, black-water stream carrying water that tasted as foul as it looked. Still, there was no likelihood that a man could die of thirst in this strange country.

Slocum was used to the idea of spreading his blankets wherever night overtook him and never giving it much thought beyond the obvious concerns of water and safety from two-legged intruders.

Here the men slung hammocks, much like those he had seen on shipboard, so they would be relatively free from snakes and insects.

One of the men shot an alligator in the stream when he went to fetch coffee water, and the whole camp—with one exception—went wild with anticipation.

Damned if they didn't cut the muscular, scaly tail off the blunt-nosed, ugly creature, skin it out, and cook it for their supper. After the wagon driver's land turtles for lunch, Slocum was beginning to wonder if these crackers knew what meat was supposed to taste like. This time he passed on the roasted reptile flesh and made his meal from cold corn bread and canned peaches. Alligator was just a bit more than he wanted to chew on in any literal fashion.

It was a miserable country day or night, he decided, and at night you had to contend not only with the heat and humidity, which were unrelenting, but also with noise. Darkness made the jungle around them come alive with strange bird calls and a fearsome whirring and chirping of insects and frogs. To say nothing of the unceasing whine and snarl—he swore some of them had fangs and growled—of the mosquitoes. At least in the house there had been mosquito netting around the beds to keep them more or less at bay. In camp there were only two choices: Cover up with the blanket and risk ending up a puddle of rancid sweat, or leave the blanket off and risk being drained of the last vestige of blood by the mosquitoes. Either was miserable.

At last Slocum didn't have to endure being bothered by unwanted company. Boyd was tired and crawled into his hammock early, and Slocum did the same out of sheer boredom as much as from his need for rest.

If he had expected to gain any measure of respect from the crackers because he was quick with a gun he would have been in for a disappointment. The men had said little to him before; now they were ignoring him completely. If he gave a shit, it would have been his tough luck. As it was, he suspended himself in the hammock, swathed his head in a fold of smelly blanket, and tried to pretend that there was no such thing as a mosquito.

He could not help, though, longing for the high, rugged, cool mountains, so far away, where the water was clear and icy cold and the wind carried the scents of old snows and a man would have to travel far and search hard to find a damned mosquito. He fell asleep thinking about sawtooth peaks and Indian women.

"Head 'em, dammit, don't let the sonuvabitch back in there."

"Yeeeeeah-yipyipyipyip!!!"

"Comin' your way, Billy. Jump her."

The work was a study in confusion, so far as Slocum could see. Noise from the crash of animals through brush and the shouts of men and the deep baying of the dogs. Horses and cattle and hounds leaping this way and that, mostly scarcely seen through the heavy green undergrowth. Whips cracking and cattle bellowing. Sheets of brown water curling into the air. Fanlike palmetto fronds slashing like knives as the horses plunged over and through them.

Yet in spite of the apparent confusion, the crackers seemed to be getting the job done.

Their whips and their dogs moved the bovines out of dense thickets where Slocum could barely *see* a damned cow much less rope one. And their homely little horses, without enough bone and muscle to drag a steer to earth, could move like cats over the soft, often slippery, root-tangled footing.

Slocum felt like a rank greenhorn for the first time in his memory.

Even Boyd seemed aware of his unsuitability for this particular task. The cracker cowboys damn sure were aware of it.

"Over there, John." Boyd was pointing across one of the rare dry-grass openings they had come upon. "Get those sons o' bitches and push 'em over into the herd here."

"Right."

Finally there was something to be done that looked like it would be up Slocum's alley. For a change, the cattle glimpsed in the distance were on high, dry ground in a stand of scrub oak instead of mired in a swampy jungle. He spurred his horse hard and took off in a run toward the scrawny, tick-infested bovines.

He skirted another of those always present mottes of cypress and stagnant water, trying to flank the cattle and drive them toward the gather the crackers were making, but the damn bovines saw him coming and slipped away into the scrub oak in an attempt to escape.

Fair enough, Slocum thought. At least chasing them he wouldn't have to buck any swamps. Hell, they could run as far as they wanted and he wouldn't mind. Not as long as they stayed on dry ground to do it.

He pulled the horse down to a lope and continued a wide, sweeping circle that he calculated should eventually put him behind the small group of cattle so he might eventually get them to drift in the direction he wanted.

Here and there, though, he had to swing out of his way to avoid a tangle or a motte. Forty-five minutes or so later, well, he was not lost. Exactly. But he was not sure in which precise direction those cattle had to be driven in order for them to reach the herd.

Every direction looked pretty much the same, he acknowledged, when you couldn't see farther than a matter of yards. He pulled his horse to a halt, cussed himself a bit, and lit a cigar.

To make matters worse, the damned cattle had decided to hole up in a hock-deep lagoon of green-scummed water and shaggy cypress trees.

"If this ain't the shits," Slocum mumbled. The scruffy pony he was riding twitched its ears at his voice and shifted patiently onto one hind leg.

"There's no way you and me are gonna get them outta there by ourselves," Slocum told the horse. "I reckon we might as well head back."

He took up the reins again and paused to squint through the overhanging screen of branches and leaves toward the sky. It had been mid-afternoon when he started this chase. Now the light was fading. He had no idea how low the sun was, since the growth was too heavy to allow him a look at it. Still, it would be dark long before Slocum would be able to find his way back to camp.

"Shit," he muttered. "Cold supper two nights in a row."

Instead of trying to retrace the roundabout route he had taken chasing the cattle, he estimated about where

the camp and the herd should be and cut straight for it.
Even so, it was nearly full dark by the time he reached
a road—a twin-tracked wagon path was more like it,
really—that ran in the general direction he was wanting
to go.

At least on a road he would not have to worry about
bad footing and frequent detours in the darkness. He
reined the horse onto the path.

It wasn't five minutes later that the bastards jumped
him.

20

Slocum ducked his head and leaned low along the neck of the horse so he could pass beneath an overhanging limb on a huge old tree. It was much too dark now for him to be able to see what kind of tree it was. Assuming he could have recognized anything in this foreign country anyway.

The next thing he knew it was like those damned mosquitoes. Except this swarm of creatures each stood about six feet tall and had a whole lot more heft than even the biggest mosquito.

At least two of them had been waiting above him in the tree, and there were more on the ground.

Dropping from above and jumping for his legs at the same time, they overwhelmed him and carried him from the saddle into the soft, sandy dirt before even his quick reflexes could bring a gun into play.

They were a blur of shadows and hard bodies, and Slocum found himself fighting for his life without a moment's notice.

He lashed out with his foot and had the satisfaction of hearing a sharp exhalation of breath and a following grunt of pain, but there were just too many of them. They pinned his arms, and others wrestled him to the ground and fell on his legs so he couldn't kick any longer.

Some sonuvabitch had a forearm locked under Slocum's jaw, pressing into his throat and cutting off his air. He felt the world beginning to gray out, and he twisted and bucked and tried for any sort of hold.

His teeth found someone's ear, and Slocum bit into the yielding cartilage with all the strength he possessed.

The man shrieked and jerked away, leaving Slocum with a mouthful of tissue and blood but damned little in the way of satisfaction.

Someone else, several someones, began to rain short, hard punches into his belly and his kidneys alternately as Slocum writhed and tried to twist away.

Someone else yelped out in pain, obviously from an attacker's missed blow because Slocum was not able to throw any punches himself. A moment later a hard object connected with Slocum's skull, and he fell limp.

He was not unconscious. Not quite. He was close enough to it to be floating in a soft, never-never land where he was totally out of the fight even though he remained aware of what was going on around him. Uninterested in it but aware of it.

"Scrappy sonuvabitch," he heard a voice say.

The men who had engulfed him began to separate and pick themselves up, their shapes towering over him in the darkness as he lay woozy and dazed on the ground at their feet.

At least now the pressure on his throat had been released, and he could breathe properly again.

Slocum told himself to bide his time and play possum while he got some strength and oxygen back into his system. It was not hard advice to take. He was incapable of doing much of anything else for the time being.

"Fetch that light over heah an' strike a light, somebody," a voice ordered. "Let's see which o' the bastahds we got heah."

There was a sound of moving feet and then the distinctive scratch of a lucifer grating against a rubbing stick. The light flared and then steadied as the lantern was lit.

Slocum squinted into the sudden light. Beyond the lantern he could make out a ring of beard-stubbled faces with the slack jaws and malarial yellow skin that was common to this country. These were not members of the Calder crew, but they were very much like them. A land of pricks and assholes, Slocum decided. He didn't feel the least bit sorry about reaching that harsh judgment.

"I ain't seen this'n before," one of them said. "Anybody else know him?"

No one spoke, although there was a general shaking of heads around the circle of faces.

"Who are ya?"

Slocum managed to sit up. He massaged his throat and took his time about answering them. "Name's Slocum," he said finally.

"That don't mean shit to me, mister," said the one who seemed to be the leader of the pack.

"It would if there wasn't quite so damned many of you," Slocum said.

He figured he already knew the answer, but he wanted to make sure. He leaned forward, hoping without hope that he might still encounter the rigid resistance of a .36 Navy Colt shape at his waistline, but as he had expected, the gun had been lost in the fight. Pity, he thought.

"Feisty bastahd, ain't you?"

"I have my moments," he said. "Even if this don't seem to be one of them."

"Uh huh. So what's your business here?"

"So what the hell is your business asking? I never had trouble with you before or you wouldn't be here to complain about it," Slocum returned.

"Uh huh. Good an' feisty, all right."

"Don't fret about it, Art," a voice called from the edge of the group. "We got all the answers we need right heah." He was a young, lanky cracker barely old enough to need a weekly shave. He stepped into the light of the lantern leading the little horse Slocum had been riding. The animal must have shied and bolted when the rush of bodies hit, but it had not gone far.

"What you got, Tommy?"

The boy jerked a thumb in Slocum's direction. "His mount. Calder's brand. That's what I got."

"Is that right, Slocum? You ridin' for Calder?"

Slocum shrugged. "Either I'm riding for the man or I stole his horse."

The leader, Art, grinned. "Of the two, mistuh, I'd

respect you more if'n you stoled his damn horse.'' He chuckled. ''O' course we'll hang you for either offense.''

''I don't suppose you'd tell a fella why?'' Slocum asked. He was trying to buy some time, trying to delay until he could find some sort of opening. Anything at all would do.

''I thought I jus' *did* tell yuh,'' Art said.

''Look . . .'' Slocum gestured with his left hand and assumed a vapid, inoffensive expression.

His right hand, while they were or should have been watching the left, flashed toward the knife sheath at his belt.

And came up empty.

''Lookin' for this?'' someone asked.

There was no point in waiting any longer. Slocum launched himself at the man closest to him and brought his fist slashing up in a crushingly hard punch into the man's gonads. The fellow screamed and went down.

But that was all there was time for.

The men, whoever they were, jumped him for the second time, and again Slocum felt himself swarmed under by the crush of bodies and pummeling fists.

There were just too many of them, and in a disgustingly short time he was spread-eagled on the ground again with a hard point of root jabbing him in the small of the back and a flow of blood coming from a split over his right eye. They were like a pack of wolves, and there was nothing he could do to keep himself from going under. He could not even take one of the bastards with him, although he tried his best.

''You can quit punchin' him now,'' Art said. Slowly the others complied.

Art grinned at him. ''We don't figure to hurt you more'n we have to, you know. Jus' hang you.''

''Mighty kind of you, I'm sure,'' Slocum said from flat on his back. Both arms and both legs were pinned firmly to the soil. He thought about trying to spit into the man's face but decided he didn't have the range for it from that angle.

"Fetch him up heah, boys."

Slocum felt himself being plucked off of the ground by a dozen willing hands. They stood him upright, and some thoughtful soul, perhaps prompted by experience, slipped a coil of braided blacksnake whip around his ankles to keep him from kicking anyone.

"I wish you hadn't done that," Slocum said drily.

"Reckon you do," the man agreed.

"Now what?" Slocum asked.

Art looked over his shoulder. One of them at the edge of the lantern light had a coil of rope in his hands and was laboring to fashion a noose.

Slocum was interested, but not particularly pleased, to see that they did that in the same efficient fashion here as on the other side of the Mississippi.

"I have an allergy to hemp," Slocum said. "I figure it's only fair to warn you about that. Sometimes the stuff even makes me pissed off."

"Aw, we'll take our chances," Art told him.

"Uh huh."

The man building the noose was slow at his task. Not that Slocum was wishing for any speed. There was a peculiar fascination, though , that made Slocum watch every movement of hand and hemp as the traditional thirteen twists were built. Slocum's mouth was dry.

"Somebody comin'," the boy named Tommy said.

The noose builder stopped what he was doing—Slocum didn't mind—and they all stood in silence to listen. There was the sound of a single horse moving down the road toward them.

One horse. That was a shame, Slocum thought. Under the circumstances he would have been plumb tickled to see Boyd Calder and his asshole cracker cowboys.

The rider reached them, and the group of men parted to make way.

Slocum looked up, and his eyes went wide. The sight that greeted him in the yellow glow of lantern light was hardly what he might have expected.

21

It was an apparition. A ghost. A spirit from the long dead past.

That was the only possible explanation. Being so close to dying himself at the end of a hangman's rope, Slocum was already beginning to see the already dead.

It had to be so.

Yet these shit-kicking crackers acted like they were seeing the same spirit. Except they seemed to regard it as a perfectly normal, everyday sort of sight.

Slocum blinked and shook his head. Nope, he didn't wake up. So he must not have been dreaming it. He looked again.

What this was, by damn, was a *lady*.

In the old-fashioned, sure enough, Deep South sense of that term. And that was saying quite a lot indeed.

This was one genuine, definite, no doubt about it *lady*. Just like he had seen them back in Vicksburg, back before Grant's unpleasantnesses there.

Even her costume was exactly as he remembered they should be. Puff sleeves. Mountains of crinolines. Lace-trimmed round bonnet. Muff dangling from the wrist—and in miserable heat like this, too. A damned muff. Lace on the dress matching the lace on the bonnet. Fabric inset on the hook-and-eye shoes matching the fabric of the dress.

Jesus! Slocum could scarcely believe it.

And of *course* she was riding sidesaddle. Was there any other way for a lady to ride? Horrors. Zounds. All that crap. He blinked and shook his head again.

That getup *had* to be old enough to have been fashionable back when things were considerably different through all of the South. Had to be. And—he looked more closely in the uncertain lantern light—its wearer was probably old enough to have worn the dress back then herself.

Although neither John Slocum nor any other man was likely to complain that the lady had not aged well in the years since.

She was . . . she was damn well beautiful, that was all there was to it. A genuine southern beauty. A belle of the first water.

Tall, obviously, and just as obviously reed-slim, no need to wear one of those corsets—Slocum remembered the time it took to unlace those damned things—with the whalebone stays and yards of cable running through the eyelets. But that had been the fashion, and Slocum would have bet any amount that beneath her gown this lady was wearing one of the things in spite of heat and current fashion and whatever else. He would have wagered any amount on that.

Her face was sunken-cheeked beneath high, prominent cheekbones, and she carried her head atop a slender, milk-white—alabaster was the archaic, poet's word that came instantly to mind when he looked at this belle from the antebellum South—neck.

She had a decidedly patrician cast to her features and a confidence about her that in anyone else he had seen would have seemed arrogance. Not in this grand lady. In her it was a calm certainty of her own value rather than any taint of arrogance.

There was a *special* quality about her, Slocum quickly decided, that went beyond her beauty.

He looked up at her, seated so easily on the back of a leggy bay horse, the best-looking animal he had seen since he left Texas; hell, since the last time he had been to Kentucky; and he felt a rush of desire for this lady. More, he felt a shyness within himself that was so rare he would have thought it impossible ever to experience such a feeling again.

Slocum swallowed hard and allowed himself to admire

the beauty of this grand lady who sat in the midst of these cracker ruffians.

The hanging party, whoever the hell they were, also recognized the quality of this woman. To a man, they took their hats off and stood silent while she looked them over, one and then another. The silence was hers to break, for none of them was likely to. Nor was John Slocum. The woman affected him that much.

"What are you about here, Arthur?" she asked in a soft voice when she was done piercing them with her eyes. Slocum was sure that this one would never find it necessary to raise her voice. Whenever she spoke she would be heard.

Art twisted the brim of his hat in strong hands and coughed slightly before he answered.

"We, uh, we was fixing to protect some private property, Miss Elizabeth. You know."

"Indeed I do know." She took one gloved hand from the reins of her proud bay and pointed her quirt toward the hangman's noose still being held by the cracker who had made it. "Have you made it well, Harold?"

The noose maker bobbed his head and stammered, "Yes'm, Miss Elizabeth. Hit'll work fine."

"You must be humane in these matters," the lady said softly. "One cannot condone the infliction of pain, with cause or without. You know this."

There was a round of nodding heads and a quick agreement with her. Slocum got the impression that the men would have agreed with nearly anything this lady said. What had they called her? Elizabeth. He tucked that knowledge away, although he had no hope of needing to know it. Not since he was about to hang.

And damn-all, he thought, this elegant lady seemed to be going right along with their hanging notions.

"Shee-it," he said aloud. The remark brought him a backhanded cuff from the nearest cracker.

"Watch yer mouth, mistuh," the man snapped. "Miss Elizabeth don't need to hear vulgarity from the likes o' you."

Slocum glared at him, the green fire dancing in his eyes, and he knew that if he had been free this man would be dead now. The cracker knew it too, and his eyes quickly fled from Slocum's stare.

Slocum stood with his head high and turned the fire of his gaze onto the woman next. A trickle of blood ran from his lips, but he ignored it. They could kill him, but they couldn't defeat him.

The soft, melodic voice filled the small, lamplit space along the roadside again. "This man does not act like most, Arthur. Are you so sure of him?"

"Yes'm."

She nodded, but although it was Art she was talking to, it was Slocum she continued to look at. She fell silent then and seemed to be in thought.

"What is your name, sir?" she asked Slocum. He told her.

"Would you happen to be the gentleman visiting from the western territories, sir?"

"I am from the West, ma'am. Whether I remain a gentleman I leave to your discretion." Slocum made a leg toward her and then snapped erect, unconsciously coming to attention as an officer and gentleman was expected to do upon being introduced to a lady.

"Pretty manners for a frontiersman, sir," she said in that gentle, liquid voice. "Might you have been more agreeably engaged in the past?"

"Indeed, ma'am." He named his unit and former commander from the time when he had worn the gray and gold.

"An honorable profession, sir."

"If no longer viable," he agreed.

The lady smiled. "There are some things I might like to ask you, sir. Would you object?"

"My time is rather completely occupied at the moment. Perhaps tomorrow?"

She laughed. She waved her quirt casually toward Harold and his hangman's knot. "Put that thing away, please. No, wait." To Slocum she said, "You no doubt are familiar with conditions of parole, sir. Would you accept them?''

"I have only my word to give as bond," Slocum said.

"Have you nothing of greater value?"

"No man has anything of greater value," Slocum said softly.

"Well spoken, then, sir. And I shall accept your word and grant the parole. Arthur, Mr. Slocum is paroled into my custody, then. He will accompany me. Thomas, if that is his mount, please deliver it into his hands. I am already late for my dinner."

"But, ma'am . . ." The boy wanted to protest, but the look she gave him held as much fire and ice as John Slocum's sternest glare. The boy clamped his mouth shut against the rest of what he might have said and turned his eyes away from hers.

Slocum, feeling as much anticipation as he did relief, gave the cracker boys a sardonic grin and stepped forward to claim the reins from Tommy's reluctant grasp.

He tossed them a salute as he swung onto the pony, and when the lady turned her handsome bay away, Slocum was at her side.

He felt no regret to be leaving that eager company behind.

22

The house she led him to was what Slocum would have expected of the Calder place, since it was supposed to be the grand spread of the countryside. This house, well illuminated inside and out by lamps and post lanterns and even a few torches, was all the woman's appearance had implied. Columns and porticoes and chimneys everywhere. Groomed lawn and trimmed plantings in neat rows along the circular drive. If a closer look showed the paint to be chipped and badly in need of restoration, well, Slocum was in no position to complain.

"Welcome to The Oaks, Captain," the woman said as they reached the front of the impressive structure.

" 'Mister' suits me better these days," Slocum said. "Or 'John.' The western country is informal at best."

"As you prefer, John."

By the time she brought the big bay to a halt there was a servant boy at her stirrup to hand her down and take the horse away. He also took Slocum's reins and led the scruffy little cow pony off into the darkness.

"I thought slavery was illegal these days," Slocum said after the boy had disappeared.

"Slavery is," she agreed. "Servitude is not. There remains a difference, you know. Besides, my people are here because they choose to be. Some of them stayed after the recent unpleasantness. And, frankly, I believe more might have returned after their fling in the harsh realities of the world beyond The Oaks except that pride would prevent their return. I know I should have been too proud to return had our situations been reversed."

Slocum raised an eyebrow. "Pride, ma'am? Reversed

situations? That sounds like your slaves were almost human.''

She gave him a scathing look. ''I am a southerner, Mr. Slocum; I am not a fool. But your remark makes me suspect that I may have misjudged all I have heard about you.''

Slocum swept his hat off and bowed. Rather elegantly for someone so far out of practice, he thought. ''My apologies, ma'am, but I wished to understand your own feelings in the matter.''

''And you, sir?''

Slocum grinned at her. ''I have lived by the gun and the knife, ma'am. It does not pay to inquire of a man's color when he is standing at your side. Just how well he can shoot.''

''Come in, then, sir. And do remember your parole, please.''

There was a glint in the woman's eye that Slocum caught, but which at first he did not recognize. It seemed so very much out of character for this elegant creature. And yet it was unmistakable. She was putting him on. And had been putting on those crackers back there too. He was sure of it.

''This parole, ma'am . . .''

''Yes?''

''You, uh, put a great deal of stock in it, do you?''

She laughed. ''Perhaps as much as you do, sir, on the frontier.''

Slocum felt himself begin to relax with this beautiful and unquestionably bright woman. He laughed with her and followed her into the tastefully appointed entry hall of The Oaks' mansion.

She led him into a parlor that was festooned with tapestries and oil paintings, poured brandy for both of them without asking, and pointed Slocum toward a deeply cushioned armchair with a heavy ottoman before it. Then, perhaps for shock effect, the grand lady flopped herself down into a matching chair and put her feet up onto the ottoman. Slocum might indeed have been taken aback if that glimmer of amusement in her eyes had not prepared him to find this woman much more than the porcelain figurine she had seemed at first glance.

Taking her unladylike posture in stride, Slocum raised his brandy snifter to her in a silent salute and then made himself comfortable in the offered chair.

The woman chuckled. "No reaction, John? I like that."

"And I like you," he said. He took a sip of the brandy. It was excellent. "May I call you"—he searched for a diminutive of Elizabeth, rejected several, made his choice, and found it perfect—"may I call you Libby?"

She threw her head back and laughed. "No one ever has. But, yes, you may indeed. In fact, I think I like it."

"And the rest of it, Libby?"

She seemed genuinely surprised that he would not already have known her name. "Ashford, of course. Elizabeth Anne Caroline Ashford, sole surviving daughter of Henry G. E. Ashford of The Oaks."

"Of course," Slocum said drily.

"But then you are not interested in ancient history, are you, John?"

"Not really."

"And you are interested in . . . ?"

He thought about that for a moment before he answered. "Easy days, exciting nights, enough money to encourage both of them. I think that about covers it."

"I believe that should cover very nearly anything."

"Yes, I believe it should," he said with a slow smile. He gave her a long, level look over the rim of the brandy snifter.

Uh huh, he thought, the first appraisal in that poor lantern light had been correct. This Libby Ashford was one helluva beautiful woman. Tall and elegant. Without her riding bonnet he could see her hair, shimmering black, piled in one of those intricate dos atop her perfectly molded head. Like the ladies of the South in distant, better times, Libby Ashford still wore her hair in a mound of tight ringlets. Slocum found himself thinking that the style had had more to recommend it than he had remembered. On this woman it still looked perfectly appropriate.

"I take it that you, uh, sometimes drop convention yourself," Slocum said.

"Obviously."

"Then may I ask a question that might be considered rude in formal society?"

"Having asked that, John, you rob the question of its crudity, whatever it might be." She paused for a second. "Well, *almost* any question. But do go ahead."

"Why did you bring me here?"

The question hung in the air for some time. She sipped at her drink and stared toward a painting on the opposite wall so long that Slocum began to wonder if she had not heard. Finally she looked at him, and again there was that bright, telltale sparkle of mischief in eyes that he could now see were a deep and unusual shade of violet, quite striking under that mass of jet hair.

"Do you want honesty, John?"

"I can generally take it."

She laughed softly. "I am on very good terms with my people, John. And they are on very good terms with their counterparts in other houses. I have, shall we say, heard tales about this visitor from the western frontier. I have heard it said that you are a hard man." She smiled. "Practically all the night long, if I can believe the stories that are being told about you and a certain young lady of questionable virtue. I was both incredulous . . . and curious. And, frankly, often without outlets for certain . . . physical and emotional drives. If you see what I mean."

"Um." Slocum returned his attention to his brandy and contemplated it for some time. He looked straight into her eyes. "I believe I do."

She nodded. "Perhaps you would care to stay the night at The Oaks?"

"I would be honored," he said.

She rose from her sprawled posture in the chair, and that quickly she was once again the elegant, proper lady. "I shall have someone show you to your room."

Slocum stood, as courtesy demanded. "Might I bother them also for facilities to bathe? I, uh, am not entirely clean."

"By all means, Mr. Slocum. And . . . perhaps I shall see you again. In the near future."

Slocum bowed. "I am sure of it."

Elizabeth Ashford curtsied and swept grandly from the parlor. Slocum felt the stirrings of an erection.

23

Slocum was both surprised and pleased. With Libby Ashford there was none of this "let's do it but pretend we didn't" nonsense. After Slocum had bathed and wrapped himself in a velveteen dressing gown he found in the wardrobe of the room that had been given him, he heard a knock at the door.

"Come in."

The door opened, and he turned, expecting to see the lady of the manor slinking in with her attention on the hallway beyond. Instead there was a chocolate-hued servant girl standing there.

"The mistress will receive you now."

Slocum nodded and concealed his surprise by gathering up his cigars and lucifers and dropping them into a pocket of the dressing gown. He thought about taking a weapon, too, but there would have been no way to manage that without the girl seeing him. And it would have been a most ungracious response to the lady's invitation. The hell with it, he thought.

The girl led him down the hallway to a set of double doors and opened them for him to enter.

Libby Ashford's bedroom suite was larger than many houses Slocum had seen and was more elegantly appointed than a New Orleans whorehouse. The furnishings and wall hangings looked to be old, but they were anything but shabby.

It was when he saw the mistress of the manor, though, that Slocum came to a standstill and let out a low, pleased whistle.

"I've always heard about southern hospitality, Libby. Now I'm beginnin' to know what all the fuss is about."

The woman was standing beside a huge, canopied bed with mosquito netting dyed a soft, golden shade to match the satin sheets and bolster cases. She was wearing a sheer, filmy peignoir of a slightly darker golden color. And nothing else. The effect, Slocum thought, was . . . stunning.

He licked his lips in anticipation.

She stood with her head held high, sharp-tipped breasts jutting forward and her long, slender legs posed as if for an artist. She beckoned him closer. "You do approve, then, John?" She laughed lightly. She needed no answer to that question. If she had, the sight of Slocum's dressing gown preceding him by a foot, just below waist level, would have been answer enough.

Slocum's throat felt dry. He had had his share of women and more for as long as he could remember, but . . .

"I approve," he said.

The door closed behind him, he allowed the robe to drop from his shoulders.

Now it was Libby Ashford's turn to stare in wide-eyed pleasure and to lick dry lips. A slim-fingered hand rose involuntarily toward her throat.

Slocum laughed. "And do you approve?"

The massive weight of his engorged meat stood proudly forward, throbbing and bouncing with every heartbeat. Libby's eyes were locked onto that sight as firmly as if she might never be able to bring herself to look away.

"I have owned stallions that were not made so well as that, John Slocum," she said.

"I take it you do approve, then."

"I do."

He moved slowly forward until his cock was pressed against her belly and her marble-hard nipples were teasing his chest. Only then did the woman raise her eyes to meet his.

Slocum took her into his muscular arms and explored the sweet depths of her mouth with his tongue. She met his explorations hungrily and thrust and parried with the heat of her own tongue. Her flesh was cool against his body, and he wanted to find and to drink of the essence of this beautiful female.

Yet for a change he was in no hurry to conclude their tryst. This he wanted to savor for as long as might be possible.

Still locked together in a slow, powerful embrace, Slocum bent and lifted her. He swung her lightly onto the bed and lay beside her without breaking their kiss.

He ran his hand over the swell of her hip and across the delicate ripples of her rib cage to the proud, firm swell of her breasts. She moaned into his mouth when he rolled her nipple between suddenly gentle fingertips, and he felt her shift on the bed, opening herself to him.

It was rare that John Slocum wanted to give as much as to take. With Rose Calder, with any of the countless readily available women with whom he passed his time, he liked to plunge into them for his own pleasure. But Libby Ashford was no ordinary woman. With this woman he wanted more.

Her thighs, as cool and smooth as the satin they lay on, were open for him, but for a few moments longer he continued to play with her nipples and to drink the breath from her mouth. Then he pulled away and began to run his tongue lightly over her.

First at the corners of her mouth, across her chin and down to the ivory column that was her throat. Libby's eyes closed, and she strained her head back to allow him better access.

He tasted of her breasts and nipped the buds of her nipples between his lips. The pattern of her breathing became heavier, and her head rolled from side to side.

Slocum licked her belly and probed with his tongue into the shallow pool of her navel.

His tongue found the soft, dark curls of her pubic hair, and he nuzzled against her there. Her fragrance was light and pleasant and invited him further.

The lips of her sex were moist and open, and the taste of her was all that the scent had implied. He began to lap at the hard, proud little jut of flesh that was her clitoris, and Libby cried out. Her hips began to writhe and gyrate in time with the slow motions of his tongue, and she sang the low, sweet song that has no words.

A moment more and he could feel her body tense. She became rigid and raised herself to him hungrily.

Her entire body vibrated and then convulsed, and she screamed aloud into the silence of the huge bedroom. Her thighs pounded against his ears, and the power of their grip threatened to strangle him. But for an instant only. A moment later she lay limp and gasping, her slim, perfectly formed body fighting for breath and her hands caressing Slocum's head.

He sighed. He would have to give her a moment to recover before she would be able to return the favor. He did not mind. He was in no hurry whatsoever.

24

Damn! She even sucked cock like a lady! No gobbling or slurping to it. Just deep and sweet and warm.

Slocum felt the fire of molten steel beginning to build toward the point of explosion in his balls. He wasn't ready. Not yet. He wanted more before he would allow himself to gush out like liquid fire. He reached down and pulled her head away.

Libby didn't question or complain. She looked at him with a catlike smile and provocatively licked her full, wet lips. Then she buried her face contentedly against his heavy, swollen balls.

Slocum toyed with the flow of dark curls and let his fingers stray down the smooth curve of her back to the velvet-textured skin of her hip and rump. He squeezed and probed the hot, moist hollows of her, sliding his fingers inside her by both avenues at one time. The ring of her sphincter muscle closed tight on the digit that was in her ass, and he could feel the narrow wall of superheated flesh that separated the joints of one finger from the other. Libby moaned and pushed back against him.

"That would be a nice place whenever you're ready, John."

Slocum nodded, not caring that her eyes were closed and she could not see the gesture. The communication between them was such that she did not need to see; she would simply *know*.

She lifted her head and bent to him again, but the sensations this woman was able to impart were so powerful that he had to stop her again after little more than a moment. Any more and he would spill his juices before he was willing.

"Now," he croaked when he could take no more.

Libby raised herself from him and stretched out belly down on the bed beside him. She lay with her legs apart, her hands pulling the cheeks of her round, lovely ass wide to ease his entry.

Slocum knelt over her and pressed the engorged tip of his massive tool at the red rosebud she was offering him. He pressed forward slowly, and her hole parted to receive him.

He slid full-length into her, and she gladly accepted the full weight of his body onto her own slender frame.

Entering her was like slipping it into a bonfire. The heat of her and the tightness took him to the limits of pleasure, sending him up onto that knife edge of sensation that is the borderline between pleasure and pain.

He could feel the tightness ease slightly as she relaxed and gave herself to an acceptance of the huge thing that now was so deep within her slim body. Slocum began to pump into her, withdrawing and sliding forward slowly and gently at first, then faster and with more power, until finally he was bucking and ramming into her wildly.

And Libby gave back to him every thrust and every grind.

Slocum's lips drew back from his teeth in a grimace that was as much snarl as it was satisfaction, and he sent what felt like a quart of steaming hot jism pouring out inside her. He clenched his teeth to keep from crying out, but even so a low, growling groan escaped from him.

He collapsed on top of her, totally spent, totally at ease now.

The night was long but hardly long enough for all they wanted to explore and examine, and in the pale light of the early dawn she slipped out of the wide bed and padded barefoot and gloriously naked to the carved and gilded table where a pitcher and basin were waiting.

Libby poured from the pitcher and wet a cloth. She washed herself and then returned to bend over Slocum's limp, utterly spent body to wash his cods and tool with tender care. When she was done—and he had to admit it made him feel better and more refreshed than he might have believed—she bent to give him a quick, friendly kiss on the head of his sore and no longer willing pecker.

"Breakfast?" She sounded as bright and cheerful as if she had just awakened from a night of joyful dreaming, although Slocum knew for a certainty that she had not slept for a moment the entire night long.

"You don't mean you're quitting," he accused, knowing full well that if she said she was not she had called his bluff and routed him as no gambler on earth had ever been able to do. He simply, and literally, was not up to any more screwing.

"Temporarily," she said.

He pretended disappointment, but he was sure that she knew as well as he did that a rest was a necessity at this point.

"You needn't be formal," she said as he swung his knobby, scarred legs off the side of the bed. "The dressing gown will be enough. There is no one here but the servants, and it would be impossible to keep a secret from them if I tried."

Slocum pulled on the finely made robe and watched with appreciation for her beauty, if no longer with any trace of lust, while Libby covered herself with a matching robe she pulled from the armoire in a corner of the room.

She paused at the mirror to brush her gleaming hair, and Slocum marveled that she, or any woman, might have come through such a vigorous night with no trace of outward effects showing to mar her beauty.

He rubbed at the stubble on his chin and made a face. If nothing else, he would have thought that every square inch of that perfect body should by now have taken on a sandpapered appearance. Yet she looked fresh and almost virginal in the strengthening morning light.

Slocum grinned. If this was a virgin, by damn, he'd take one every time.

Libby led him down the hallway past the room that in theory was his, to the curving staircase that led to the main floor below. The formal dining table, long enough to accommodate at least a score of guests, was already laid with places for two, and the servant girl Slocum had seen the previous evening was waiting for them with a smile and a bowl of freshly cut red and yellow flowers of a kind Slocum had never seen before.

Slocum seated Libby and found himself being helped to his chair by the girl who, he guessed, must have been a former slave, although she was young enough that she might have little or no memory of that form of servitude.

It was, he admitted, an odd feeling to have his chair held for him by a polite and not unattractive girl who, under other circumstances, he might have been trying to tumble. A man finds himself in odd and sometimes wondrous surroundings, Slocum thought, when he chooses to follow the roads that do *not* carry signposts reading SECURITY and RESPECTABILITY. He sighed.

Coffee was served immediately, and fried pork and hominy were not long behind. They ate in silence, Slocum wolfing the meal with relish and Libby picking daintily at this and that, as no doubt she had been taught a lady should. Only when they were done and the table cleared down to the cups and saucers did either of them speak again.

"We, uh, haven't actually gotten around to discussing the terms of my parole," Slocum observed. He pushed his chair back from the table and stretched his legs. As if she had been reading his mind, the serving girl appeared at his elbow with a dry and obviously old but fine cigar. She trimmed it for him and held a lighted match until Slocum had a satisfactory glow going.

"But I thought we did," Libby said. She was smiling.

"Really?"

She laughed. "I think it fair to say that you have satisfied the conditions of parole thus far, John."

"If that's so, why, I'll be proud to be your prisoner anytime you wish, Mistress Ashford."

"La, sir, you flatter me."

"Seriously," Slocum said, "you, uh, you don't really put much stock in that stuff anymore, do you?"

She chuckled. "Lordy, John. Of *course* not."

"But weren't you taking an awful chance, bringing me here, not even taking my gun away? I mean, I could have been any sort of scoundrel. You couldn't know that."

Again she laughed, although he had no idea what she might be finding to amuse her in such a warning. She was beautiful and she was competent, sure, but she would be no match for any reasonably healthy male who wanted to do more than enjoy a romp between those lovely thighs. A man bent on robbery, or one of those who got his jollies from blood and pain, would offer her no chance at all.

"I was perfectly safe, I assure you."

"Lookahere, Libby," Slocum began. "I like you, dammit, and I'm tellin' you there are some bad dudes in this here world. Why—"

She was laughing quite loudly now. "Oh, John. Dear John. You are a woolly bear of a man but really quite sweet and thoughtful."

"Dammit, Libby, I'm serious about this, and—"

"Hush, dear. I know you are. But there are things that you do *not* know, also." She paused and chuckled. After a moment she turned her head and called out, "Lem."

The door to the kitchen swung open, but there was damn little light that was able to pass through it. Nearly the entire opening was blocked by the hulking frame of a tall, coal-black man with shoulders that would barely fit through a normal doorway and a chest as thick as a flour barrel.

He was barefoot and bare-chested, and Slocum could find not an ounce of fat anywhere on him. His chest and arms and belly were corded with slabs of muscle, and his ebony skin had the oily sheen of superb health and conditioning.

The man reminded Slocum of some kind of jungle animal, not a man at all. Perhaps one of those black jungle cats that Slocum had seen pictures of in some book.

Lem carried a broad-bladed cane knife in a sash at his waist, although Slocum could not imagine any human opponent powerful enough that the former slave might fine the need for such a weapon. Or for any weapon at all. He looked perfectly capable of strangling an ox with his bare hands.

For sure Slocum would not want to have to face him. Not with an ax or even a fucking Colt .45. A three-pound howitzer maybe. And that would be somewhere on the light side of safety.

Shee-it, Slocum thought.

Libby Ashford gave Slocum a tight little smile. "That, John, is the reason I need have no fear for my safety. Lem is always within the sound of my voice. He has been for as long as I can remember." She turned to face the ebony giant. "Thank you, Lem."

The huge black grinned, yellow teeth gleaming in the polished coal of his face, and bobbed his head. "Mist'ess." He backed away and allowed the door to swing shut.

Slocum found himself letting out a breath he had not realized he was holding in.

Damn, he thought, it pays to be a good boy around here. That big bastard was enough to make a man run from The Oaks screaming and hollering.

He looked over at Libby, coolly beautiful and poised at her table.

On the other hand, Slocum reflected, there were some reasons for staying, too.

25

"We thought you was dead. Or had mebbe run out on us." Old man Calder sounded less than enthusiastic in his welcome. More accusing than welcoming, actually.

Not that Slocum gave a shit. After four days, and four nights, with Libby Ashford, what he wanted more than a welcome was a chance to hit the bunk and sleep the damn clock around. He was about as pussy-whipped as he had ever been in his life.

"What happened?" Boyd Calder's father demanded.

Slocum told him over his shoulder while he unsaddled the rough but sturdy little pony that had carried him back. At least, Slocum told him *some* of what had happened in the last few days.

"Anyway," Slocum concluded, "I don't know who the bastards were nor what they wanted. When the lady offered me a place to rest up from the pounding, I took it. Wouldn't've been proper to say no to her after what she had done."

"Ashford, huh," Calder said with a grunt of disgust. "If that high and mighty bitch took you in, she's up to something, and that's the gospel. Can't trust none of that kind nor none of that crowd, neither one. Bitch," he repeated.

Slocum had a somewhat different opinion of the lady himself, but he remained silent.

Actually, the only reason he had come back to the Calder place at all was not from any sense of loyalty toward the family—certainly not toward the Calder riding crew—but a matter of simple need. Calder had hired him and had the money to pay him for his services. Libby Ashford was old-family pride without the resources nowadays to maintain the life-style that should have been hers. She was broke. And therefore John Slocum could not afford to stay there. Not if he expected to get back to Texas, he didn't.

That, though, was the *only* reason he had been willing to come back to the Calder spread.

He turned the cow pony into the corral and carried his borrowed saddle and bridle into the shed. Even that was different in this benighted, godforsaken, miserable collection of mold and mildew. A man couldn't even throw his saddle on a fence rail here. If you did, you'd end up with a bunch of green, rotting slime where the leather ought to be. You had to store the damn things under cover or they would rot away to nothing. What it came right down to was that John Slocum was not particularly enamored with Florida this evening. He wanted to be back in country that he understood. Or back in Libby Ashford's bed. He was not entirely sure which.

"I told ya," a voice said behind him.

Calder grunted.

Slocum turned. Some of the hands had drifted over after he rode in and began talking to the boss man. Now he saw that Honus Luther was among them and had shoved to the front of the pack. As far as Slocum was concerned they were all a bunch of pricks, and the quicker he could get away from here the better.

"You say something?" he demanded, staring Luther in the eyes and more than half hoping the man would give him cause for action. That Colt Navy was still in his belt, and he would have been happy for an excuse to turn it loose.

Luther's eyes shifted away from Slocum's and sought the toes of his tattered shoes. "I thought I seen your horse over at the bitch's place, that's all," he mumbled. "Tol' the boss that th' other day. Reckon I was right."

"What of it?" Slocum demanded.

"Nothin'. Jus' that I was right." Luther looked past Slocum toward the corral, glanced down again and began studying his nails, shifted from one foot to the other. There was no fight in him, Slocum saw. Pity.

"Was there something else, then?" Slocum asked of Calder.

He shook his head. "I guess not. Supper oughta be about ready."

Slocum nodded. He turned his back on the crew and walked ahead of Calder toward the family house. After The Oaks, the place looked shabbier than ever.

If Calder and the men had been unimpressed with Slocum's return from a hangman's noose, Boyd was ecstatic. As soon as he saw Slocum enter the room he jumped to his feet and ran to grab Slocum by the arms.

Rose too had a quick leap of joy in her eyes when she saw the tall westerner, although she had to refrain from any outward show of her welcome.

Slocum saw her reaction, though, and groaned softly to himself. If there was anything he wanted this night it was not a passionate encounter. He wanted to be left alone to get some sleep and let his gonads build up some more juices before any woman went to draining them off again.

Besides, after the sleek elegance of Libby Ashford, Rose Calder looked pasty and doughy. Not unhealthy exactly, but not desirable either. He wondered if there would be any way to avoid the damned girl after supper.

He gave his attention to Boyd, who was excitedly pumping him for details of the experience he had gone through.

For Slocum the scrap on the road that night was distant past history, and he had to search his memory to try to satisfy the boy's curiosity. About Libby he said little, although under Boyd's questioning that was easy. The kid was interested in wild and woolly action and seemed not to care about what might have happened afterward.

Boyd kept him busy talking through dinner and in the parlor long afterward. Which was all right by Slocum. Eventually Rose had to leave the conversation or it would have been obvious where her interest lay. As soon as she was gone Slocum admitted to the Calder family that he was weary and excused himself.

With any luck, he thought, he would be able to sleep through the night for a change.

He found his way to his bedroom, locked the door behind him, and managed to strip before he collapsed into the lumpy bed.

The sheets, he noticed before he slept, still stank of sweat and cum from the exercises he and Rose had performed there.

Things were definitely better at The Oaks, he thought.

Libby Ashford's proud, firm body was in his mind's eye as he drifted into the sleep he so badly needed.

26

The first place Honus Luther's eyes went when Slocum appeared at the corral the next morning was to Slocum's waistband. The man probably expected that Calder would have reclaimed his .36 Navy, Slocum guessed, and he was right. The old man had requested its return that morning before breakfast, and Slocum had had no choice but to comply.

When he saw that Slocum was unarmed except for the knife that everyone carried, he grinned. "Looks like things is more equal now," he said.

Luther flexed powerful shoulder muscles and kneaded a huge right fist in his left hand.

Luther was a big man. Not in the same category with Libby Ashford's tame ape, Lem, but big nonetheless. He was half a head taller than most of the crackers Slocum had seen, and while the majority of the men around here seemed to be strung out and scrawny, perhaps because of malaria and poor food and generations of inbreeding, Luther was solidly built from one end of his frame to the other. He stood as tall as Slocum—which not too many could claim—and was much thicker through the trunk and shoulders. He looked, Slocum thought, like a man who enjoyed a fight.

"Something on your mind, Honus?"

"Damn straight there is," Luther said. "Yestidy you was lordin' it over everybody 'cause you had a gun in your belt. Well today you ain't got that advantage. Today it's just you an' me, mistuh. An' the fact is, I'm a better man than you."

Slocum laughed in the man's face. "That'll be the day."

"Name it, asshole," Luther challenged. "Knives, fists, or whips, I'll beat you any way you call it."

Slocum saw absolutely no reason to be polite and easygoing when some sonuvabitch insisted on ruining his own looks. And the choice of how to fight him was easy too. With a whip, Slocum was a babe among grown-ups compared with these dumb crackers who had grown up with a blacksnake in their hands. With a knife, Slocum would easily come out the victor—he was absolutely sure of that—but there might well be some unwelcome attention paid to him by the law if he sliced Honus Luther's gut open and fertilized Calder's poor-sand soil with a couple of gallons of fresh blood. That, Slocum could do without. Which left one choice.

Slocum grinned at Luther, dropped his right shoulder to get the big fellow's attention, and slapped him with his open left hand. The slap undoubtedly stung, landing across Luther's nose as it had done; but much more than that, it was an insulting blow. A man might slap a woman or a kid. But a grown man? The implication about what Slocum thought of Honus Luther was plain for all to see.

"That's my choice," Slocum said cheerfully.

Luther bowed his neck and would have charged straight for Slocum's belly—which was exactly what Slocum was hoping he would do; Slocum was poised and ready to finish it with one crushing blow—but two of the other hands grabbed him and held him back.

"Dammit, Honus, get y'self set or thet sneaky, stuck-up sonuvabitch'll stomp you 'fore you get inta the fight," one of the men cautioned.

"Better yet," Slocum added, "walk away while you still can."

Luther roared and shook off his two friends. He might still have bulled his way forward except that Boyd Calder chose that moment to come rushing into the group, excited and babbling at them.

"Wait a minute, boys, wait up," the kid was saying. "Hold up theah. If you gonna do this, do it right, heah?

Give the othuh boys a chanct to gathuh round an' have at it proper. You heah?''

Slocum shook his head. This kid had some strange ideas about the way grown men ought to fight. Like it was some kind of a damned game instead of the serious business of one man whipping another's ass.

And the other time Slocum had squared off with Honus Luther, the kid had made a game of death itself. That was an attitude John Slocum couldn't find it in himself to understand, much less agree with. Slocum wondered if Boyd Calder had ever had to face death himself. But, then, there was no doubt about that, was there, he quickly decided. The kid never had. Slocum sighed. Some day the stupid kid might get himself shot for his ignorance.

"What is it you have in mind, Boyd?" he asked.

"Petey, Reb, go git the other boys out heah. Leon, I want you t' shift them horses into the other pen. We'll make this corral here into a ring, sort of. They c'n fight it out man t' man there. Prize-fight rules. A round lasts till one man is down. One minute rest between. It's ovuh when one of 'em can't toe the mark for the start o' the next round.''

Boyd was as cheerful and excited as a ten-year-old on Christmas Eve.

"That all right with you boys?" he finally got around to inquiring.

Luther grunted a grudging agreement. Slocum merely shrugged his shoulders. If things had gone their natural course, he figured it would already have been over by now. Since they had not, it really didn't matter to him how Boyd wanted to dress it up for his own entertainment.

"Good, fine. Get on with it now, boys. Get 'em around.''

The rest of the damned crackers came at a run once they heard they might have a chance to see the westerner get his butt kicked, and it took no more time for the corral to be cleared.

The footing inside the pole enclosure was lousy, Slocum saw, but then the footing in this whole damned part of the country was soft and uncertain as far as Slocum had been able to determine. The whole country seemed to be made of sand and not a thing more substantial than that.

There were also more than a few piles of horse apples in the pen, some of them covered with greenish gray mold and some soft and brown and fresh. The man who went down in one of those was going to need a long, hot bath before he would be fit for human companionship, Slocum realized.

Other than those two minor points, though, he had no cause for complaint. And Honus Luther's footing would be just as bad as Slocum's.

"Any ol' time," Slocum said.

Apparently Boyd had appointed himself referee for the affair. He led both combatants into the "ring" and assigned each of them a corner.

"You're each entitled to a second," the kid said.

Luther had as many volunteers as there were cracker cowboys at the ringside. Slocum was not particularly surprised to find that none of them jumped forward into his corner. On the other hand, he wouldn't have wanted any of them there. One of them would have been as likely to do him damage as Luther.

"We need a bell, dammit," Boyd said. "Jimmy, go fetch me a hammer an' the cook's triangle." He searched in his pockets and found a turnip-sized watch he could use to time the intermission between rounds. "We're all set, then," he said when the cowboy got back with the "bell." "You boys ready?"

Both Slocum and Luther nodded.

"All right, then. Here's the rules. There'll be no bitin' nor gougin' nor head butts. No kicking nor rasslin'. Once a man's down, that round's ovuh an' the other fella's to head for his corner. No hittin' nor kickin' nor whatever when a man's on the ground. You got that?"

Luther nodded quite seriously. Slocum spat into the

dusty sand of the ring floor. It was all the same stuff that was piled on the ground at Boyd's feet as far as he was concerned.

"All right, then." Boyd made a show of dragging his heel along the ground in the approximate center of the ring. "That theah's the mark you each got to toe at the start o' each round. Now measure up to it, boys, an' we'll get started."

Slocum glanced at the men who were perched on the top rails of the pen. Usually, whenever there was a fight in order you would expect a bunch of cowhands, western or cracker either one, to be making some bets on the outcome. But not here. Not this fight. Here every damn one of them was pulling for Honus Luther, and not a one was willing to place his money elsewhere.

Slocum had a thought and turned to the crackers nearest his corner. "Anybody wanta make a small wager?"

"You damn well betcha," several responded quickly.

"I got twenty dollars." It was all the money Slocum had, the same double eagle Boyd had paid him the day they had met. "I'll stake it all if the odds are right."

"Odds?"

"It's my whole poke. An' you boys seem awful certain of the outcome here."

One of them grinned. "We seen Honus fight. You ain't."

"True. So what'll you offer."

"Two to one?" one of them said uncertainly.

"I'll . . ." Slocum would have argued the point hoping for a better offer, but Boyd began to clang on the iron triangle for them to approach the mark. "I'll take it," Slocum said.

He left the cowboys behind him arguing about which of them was to have how much of Slocum's money. That was for them to worry about. Slocum flexed his arms and rolled his head to loosen his muscles. He ignored the cowboys and walked catlike toward the center of the pen where Boyd and Luther were already waiting for him.

"I thought you was already tryin' to yellow out," Luther said.

Slocum grinned. "Let's see if you still think that when we're done."

Boyd was rubbing his hands together in his excitement. "Up to the mark now, boys, toe the mark." He backed away.

In a loud, shrill voice he called, "*Box*!"

27

Slocum was more than half expecting Luther to try to finish him immediately with a wild, bullish rush forward, but the man had had time to cool off from his earlier reactions, and it became apparent that he was not exactly a stranger to the fine art of fistfighting.

Instead of a lot of mad swinging and rushing, Luther hunched his shoulders and tucked his chin down toward his chest. He held his fists cocked before him the way Slocum had seen prizefighters do.

"Very pretty form," Slocum complimented him.

The unexpected conversation, coming when there should have been a punch instead, seemed to baffle Luther for a moment. His eyebrows went up and his guard went down.

With a smile, Slocum threw a sharp right lead that sailed in over top of Luther's guarding left and caught the man high on his left cheekbone.

"First blood to John," Boyd's voice called out from somewhere nearby—Slocum certainly was not willing to turn and look, nor did he particularly care—and sure enough there was a flow of bright blood coursing down Luther's cheek already. The skin had split slightly where Slocum tagged him.

Still, he had not gone down and did not even seem to be very much affected by the punch.

Luther ignored the blood and shuffled sideways, trying to circle Slocum and position him facing the bright ball of yellow sun just above the treetops.

Nice try, Slocum thought. He stepped sideways to meet Luther's movement and whipped an underhand left beneath Luther's high guard. The punch caught the man in the pit of the stomach. Slocum could hear the breath whistle past Luther's teeth, but he did not double over. That would have given Slocum just the opening he wanted, but Luther avoided it.

Easy. Dead easy, Slocum was thinking.

Luther's left pawed forward in short, lumbering jabs that Slocum did not even have to block to counter. He just swayed his head from side to side and let Luther's pathetically slow punches travel past without harm.

Oh, yes, Slocum thought. Easy.

Right.

It was a right, all right, and it came out of nowhere. Those slow, soft jabs had been intended to set Slocum up, and they worked. Honus Luther's right was quick and clean and businesslike, and it rocked Slocum from his skull down to the soles of his feet.

Slocum fended off the flurry of lefts and rights that followed, using his wrists and forearms to deflect the rain of blows as he shook his head and tried to pick up the rhythm of Luther's fighting.

"You're a prick, Luther, but you can punch better'n I gave you credit for," Slocum hissed.

"Punch? Shit, man, I'm just playin' with you so far."

As if to emphasize what he was saying, Luther drew back and launched a right that could have snatched Slocum's head off his shoulders if it had landed.

Slocum saw it coming and slipped away to his left, stepping inside Luther's guard while the man was out of position and smashing a combination into his gut.

Again Slocum could hear the rush of breath being driven past Luther's clenched teeth, but again there was no visible effect beyond that.

The sonuvabitch was tough, Slocum admitted. Tougher than Slocum had thought.

Respectful of each other now, the two men circled and shuffled, each trying to get the sun in the other's eyes and each wary of the power in front of him.

Around them the cracker cowboys began to yell and jeer, wanting action instead of this slow, wary dance.

If it was punching they wanted . . . Slocum feinted a right lead and threw a sizzling left that snapped Luther's head back. He followed it with a right to the belly and another high, hard left.

This was more like it, Slocum thought. He stepped in.

Luther, trying to block the punch that he thought was coming, threw his arm up and tried to sidestep at the same time. His feet tangled in the soft, sandy footing, and he fell. It was anything but a knockdown, but still Boyd jumped between them yelling, "Time, boys, end o' the round," before Slocum could move in and nail Luther again.

"Shit," Slocum muttered. He went back to his corner and lounged against the corner post, waiting for Boyd to quit playing with his damn watch and triangle.

Boyd counted off the seconds, his lips moving as he numbered them to himself. His hand rose and fell, and the hammer stroked the iron. "Toe the mark."

Slocum nodded unconsciously. He was lucky he did so. His head had moved only a fraction of an inch, but it was enough.

From behind him one of the crackers on the top rail kicked him in the head before he could move out of his corner. The toe of the fellow's shoe caught Slocum behind the ear with dizzying force. If he hadn't already been moving, the kick might have knocked him out.

No one else seemed to have seen the foul. Or at least no one who objected. Boyd Calder was looking the other way. All the rest of them would have been delighted to see Slocum on his knees, no matter how he got there.

Slocum shook his head and staggered out of the prick's reach. He was feeling slightly faint as he reached the mark Boyd had scuffed in the sand.

And Luther knew it. The bastard was grinning. He had been watching the whole thing and obviously knew that Slocum had been softened, possibly for the kill.

"Ready?" he taunted.

"Any ol' time," Slocum said. He hoped he sounded better than he felt.

Boyd, knowing nothing about what had gone on behind his back, tapped the triangle and stepped out of their way. The second round was under way.

Slocum immediately bicycled backward-out of the flurry that Luther began the instant Boyd touched his triangle.

Slocum was feeling woozy, and if Luther got to him now he might not have time to recover.

He backed swiftly away, Luther loping and shuffling after him.

"Is this a fight or a fuckin' race?" one of the crackers called derisively from ringside.

Piss on you, Slocum thought. He continued to back and to sidestep, keeping his guard up and shaking his head. He needed time. He really needed . . .

He did not have that much time. Luther guessed right about which way Slocum was about to step, got there before him, and managed to land a glancing but very hard left. Normally a punch like that would have been mildly annoying. Now it was enough to buckle Slocum's knees and send him down.

"Finish him, finish him," the men were shrieking.

But Boyd was there, jumping between them, shepherding Luther back toward his corner.

Thanks, Slocum muttered to himself. He came to his feet and stood bent over at the waist, allowing his head to clear. He stood upright and drew in several deep breaths. He flexed his shoulder muscles and swung his arms. Better. Definitely better.

He walked back toward his corner and grinned at the cowboy who had kicked him. "Good strategy," he said. "I take it you got some of the bet?"

The cowboy grinned back at him and nodded.

"Fair enough," Slocum said, "but I reckon I got to look out for my end of the wager, ol' son."

The cowboy was in the middle of an agreeing nod

when Slocum formed a fist and drove his extended knuckles into the cracker's crotch. The fellow had been sitting on the top rail with his knees apart, and the positioning was perfect. The punch caught him square on the nuts, and he turned a fishbelly white before he toppled backward off the rail to land in a moaning heap in some fresh horseshit on the ground.

"I really prefer to be left alone," Slocum said mildly.

The other crackers on the rail nearby looked away. Hadn't seen nor done a thing, they hadn't. But Slocum noticed, to give them their due, that they were not jumping down to assist the cheating cowboy who had just taken a bite out of a horse apple either.

Boyd clanged his bell, and Slocum turned to head back for the mark. This time there was no activity at his back.

"Box."

Luther was feeling confident now. He had his man groggy—if with a little help—and there would be no point in prolonging the fight. After all, there was a day's work to be done as soon as the fun was over. He stepped forward ready to put Slocum away.

John Slocum, though, was not exactly ready to be put down.

He let Luther come in, using Luther's own trick and deliberately making his jabs and parries little more than a feeble pawing at the heavy, humid air.

Luther shot out a left and another and a right-left-right combination. He was smiling. Slocum was unable to block the blows, and if he was managing to slip them with darting movements of his head, why, that was just a matter of luck. Surely it would be only a matter of time before one of those fine, powerful blows found their mark. Surely it would be . . .

Slocum's right guard fell as he swayed aside from one of Luther's punches. Neither Luther nor any of the spectators seemed to notice that the fallen guard had become a primed and ready bombshell.

They did not notice either that Slocum took the time to carefully plant his feet and set his weight.

The right drove forward without warning, and all of Slocum's strength and weight were behind it.

The fist connected with a dull *splat* flush on Honus Luther's jaw, and the big man's eyes rolled back in his head.

He was out before his suddenly boneless knees touched the ground, and he swayed forward to drop on his face without ever making a move to catch or brace himself against the fall.

The pity, Slocum thought, was that he had not fallen into a pile of shit like the other one had.

Slocum turned away. There seemed little point in waiting to see if Luther was going to toe the mark for another round. He wasn't.

And Slocum had some money to collect. That would make sixty dollars in his kick. He wondered if it would be enough to get him the hell out of this country and back to Texas where he belonged.

28

Rose Calder trailed her fingernails lightly across Slocum's naked belly and followed that touch with her tongue. Her large, globular breasts were pressed warmly against him. Libby Ashford was something special. But Rose was here. Slocum lay back and enjoyed it.

She raised her head and dragged flowing, honey-colored hair across him. "I heard you had some trouble today," she said, smiling.

"No trouble," Slocum told her curtly.

She sat up and examined him with her eyes and her fingertips. "I certainly don't see any damage."

"Did you want to?"

"No," she said quickly.

Slocum thought she said it perhaps *too* quickly. "I suspect that for some twisted reason you'd enjoy seeing me taken down a peg." Not hurt so badly that he couldn't get it up, mind, but nastied around enough to make him dependent on her.

Rose scowled at this.

Yes, he thought, that might well be what she would want.

There was something about this girl that made him want to dominate and use her. And he suspected there was something about him that made her want to sink some claws into his active flesh just as much.

Certainly he was attracted to her. She was good to look at and good as well to rut upon. But there was undeniably that spark between them that went further than a simple fuck. He wanted to . . . he did not know *what* he wanted of her. Or she of him.

He reached out and took one of those huge, firm breasts into his hand.

John Slocum's powerful hand had been as gentle as a clawless kitten with Libby Ashford's slim, elegant body. But Rose Calder was not Libby, and Slocum felt a wave of heat surge through him when he cupped that melon-sized breast in his broad palm. He felt a lust and a power that were close to rage.

He squeezed and kneaded the soft tit that overflowed his hand, and the girl's eyes closed and her lips parted in response. She pressed the weight of her chest deeper into his hand.

Slocum squeezed harder and after a moment applied his full strength in that grip. He tried his very best to mash that tender tit into a wad of mush in the palm of his hand, and Rose's head jerked in pain. She cried out softly, and he could see the glint of fresh tears welling under closed eyelids.

"You'd like it if someone here was man enough to whip me, wouldn't you?" he accused.

"No," she said. She opened her eyes then and looked at him. Her expression flickered from pain to fury. "Yes," she hissed. "I would like that."

"You'll never see that."

"Damn you, John Slocum." She dug her fingers into his arm. "Damn you."

"But you want it as much as I do. You like to be fucked the way I do it to you."

"Yes," she hissed again. "You bastard."

"Tell me."

"You sonuvabitch."

"Tell me." He pried away her hand and twisted it. For a moment neither of them moved. Then she opened her mouth and lunged forward onto him, gobbling his cock, slurping and sucking and ramming her face violently down onto him until her nose was pressed against his balls and her chin jammed sharply against Slocum's belly while she engulfed him in her throat. Her shoulders jerked as she sucked him with an awesome force that threatened to tear his meat out at the roots.

When she bared her teeth and began to savage the base of his cock, Slocum reacted as she must have known he would.

He sat up instantly and grabbed her by the hair, ripping her loose from the grip she had on him with mouth and teeth and snatching her forcibly away. He hit her then. He slapped her across the face with a full swing of his left arm while his right hand continued its grip in her hair, forcing her head into position for the blow with her face upraised and violent sobs racking her frame.

Her already flushed face turned a bright scarlet across the entire right side, and a trickle of blood showed at the corner of her full but now pale lips.

Savagely, overcome by a passion that was beyond control, Slocum flung her down onto the bed. He clamped each soft, white leg in a powerful hand and wrenched her thighs wide. Rose drew him to her eagerly. He scrambled to mount her, and he grabbed one large, pendulous breast in each hand, squeezing with all the immense force he possessed as he plunged his throbbing cock deep within her.

He bucked and rutted in her like a wild mustang stallion and tried to rip her belly open with the force of his repeated lunges. He had at that instant a mad desire to mingle her blood with his cum, and he tore into her body with the force of a whirlwind.

Rose gasped and tore at his shoulders, but her broad, receptive hips rose to meet his every plunge, and her gasps came in time with his pumping body. And when— it took no more than seconds, nor could any human body have withstood such an assault for more than seconds—Slocum exploded a flood of hot jism into her, Rose cried out in an ecstasy of her own and bit down on her underlip until another brilliant red stain of bright blood showed. She cried out loudly with the force of her climax, uncaring that anyone in the house might hear the sounds of her passion.

Slocum collapsed on top of her, drained of all emotion, and she lay beneath him as still as a corpse. She had fainted.

And Slocum himself had come closer to it than he ever wanted to again.

He thought about withdrawing from this strange, wild, beautiful young woman's body, but he didn't have the strength to pull his now limp member from her and roll off to the side. Both of them lay as they had fallen, Slocum's hard, male body collapsed on top of the soft, woman-swell of her form.

They slept.

29

"Do you know what my stupid sister did last night?"

"Huh uh," Slocum answered. He took another bite of cold corn pone and waited patiently for Boyd to go on. The two of them were seated on a rotting log at the edge of another of those interminable swamps that seemed to comprise the rangeland here. The rest of the crew sat apart from the owner's son and the stranger from the western lands and talked among themselves through the lunch break.

"The silly thing got up some time during the night. Lookin' for the thunder-mug I reckon, though she didn't say so. Anyhow, what she done was to walk smack into the side of her wardrobe." Boyd chuckled. "She looks like a mess this mornin'. Face all bruised and swole up. She's a mess all right. That's why she wasn't at breakfast. You oughta see her though. You'd laugh as loud as I did."

"Oh, I wouldn't laugh at her," Slocum said sincerely. "That wouldn't be polite."

"Yeah, well . . ." Boyd's voice died away and he took a huge mouthful of the cold, boiled pork that had been packed for their nooning. Slocum had about had a bellyful, both literally and figuratively, of boiled meat and pone. He hadn't eaten so poorly since he'd worn a gray uniform. And that had been quite a while now.

"Tell me something, rooster."

The boy's eyes brightened. Over the past few days Slocum had taken to calling the youngster that, and it seemed to please him to have a nickname given to him by a real westerner. And Slocum thought it sort of fit. If Warren Calder reminded him of a weasel, Boyd reminded him of a damned banty rooster, always charging in nine directions at once and seldom knowing what he was doing.

"Yeah?" Boyd invited eagerly.

"Those boys that was wanting to hang a Calder cowboy the other day. Nobody ever has got around to tellin' me what that's all about. And when somebody comes that close, well, it kinda makes a fella curious, if you know what I mean."

"Yeah, well, Pa don't like us to talk about it much."

"I think I'm kinda entitled, rooster."

"I expect you are at that," Boyd agreed. "The thing is, there's a bunch of damn squatters down that way, an' they resent us cause we got so many head an' we need enough graze to fatten 'em all. These squatters, they're a bunch o' white trash is what they are. Got no rights to the grazin', mind. Hell, it's all open range 'cept for a spot or two where Confederate land scrip was turned in to prove up ownership, and that sure as hell wasn't much. We got the cattle and the need, so we got the right to the use of the ground, you see. But them squatters, they resent us cause we got more than they do. That's about what it comes down to."

Slocum chewed on that for a moment. "From what I saw of Miz Ashford's place, I don't reckon I would think of her as a squatter."

"Oh, she ain't one of them. Not exactly. Hell, she ain't got hardly any cows anymore. That place used to be *some*, the way I hear, back before the war. O' course, that's what I'm told. I don't remember it my own self. Anyway, nowadays she's got that house and a couple head o' poor-blood stock and that's about all. Pa don't know how she's held out down there as long as she has. Reckon she'll go under one of these days. Kind of a shame in a way. But then, these old families can't keep going on appearances alone. You gotta grow and change with the times, that's what Pa says."

"And these squatters. Did they come in after the war?"

Boyd shrugged. "Not really. Some of 'em been around a long time. Since back during the Indian wars. They just never was worth a shit. Never will be, Pa says."

"Hell, I didn't know you'd had Indian wars down here."

"Sure. Twenty, thirty years of it off an' on. I don't remember none of it myself, but the older folks talk like it was pretty rough. Them Seminoles was pretty sneaky sons o' bitches, the way I hear it."

"Yeah," Slocum said, "all Indians are sneaky sons of bitches when it's the fella who's fought with them that's telling the story."

Slocum's dry tone of voice breezed past Boyd without getting the kid's attention, but Slocum was thinking back to some Indians he had known in the past. There were some he had fought with and more than a few he had killed. There were others he had lived with a time or two. He had about come to the conclusion that there are two sides to any fight, and a man's sympathies can depend an awful lot on which point of view he starts out seeing.

"These squatters, though," Slocum said, returning to his original question, "have they caused you much trouble?"

Boyd shrugged. "They put their whips to a couple of our boys once. An' "—he stopped and looked around to make sure no one was listening—"you won't say anything to nobody?"

Slocum shook his head.

"We ain't exactly tenderhearted city folks down here, you know. I mean, you always hear stories about the way things are out in your part o' the country. But we got our rough times too, you know."

Slocum nodded.

"Yeah, well, after they bullwhipped our boys that time, we laid up in the scrub for 'em. Caught two o' the bastards and strung 'em up from a good, big oak, we did."

"That oughta show them something," Slocum said.

"You bet," Boyd said enthusiastically. "Shows 'em we mean business, by damn. They'd best step aside when a Calder hand rides out. That's what it shows them."

"Uh huh," Slocum said. "They won't bother any Calder cowboys anymore."

"Right."

The boy seemed not to remember that some of those squatters had just tried to hang a Calder cowboy.

Slocum shook his head at the kid's ignorance. No one ever seemed to understand—or maybe it was that they weren't willing to admit—that a fight, once started, is going to go on until one side or the other is dead or in irons or until *both* sides make a truce. And that it really only takes *one* side to make a fight.

Slocum chuckled softly to himself. Funny, he reflected. Funny thing was, somehow when one side was accused of doing all the fighting, it was always the *other* side that was doing it.

After meeting Libby Ashford, Slocum was wondering just what the other side of this particular coin looked like. It was for damn sure there was another side. He just didn't happen to know what it was.

"I think," Slocum said, "I'd like a couple days off. You know, to kinda rest up from that near hanging. Do you think your pa would mind?"

"Oh, hell, John, I'm sure it'd be all right. Why, I'll give you the time myself."

Slocum nodded. "Thanks, rooster." He reached into his pocket for the unsmoked stub of a cigar he had started after breakfast. He thought he might have time to finish it before they began the afternoon's work.

30

The dinner was excellent. Bite-sized bits of venison lightly floured and fried, greens, yams, several vegetable dishes and casseroles that Slocum did not recognize, even a green salad. Libby Ashford might be poor by Boyd Calder's standards, but she certainly set a far finer table from the things that were available to her in the swamps and gardens that surrounded The Oaks. And the meal had not been prepared just because there would be a guest at the table. He had arrived too soon before dining for that to have been possible. He wiped his lips with one of the fine linen napkins and shifted his chair slightly away from the polished wood of the long table.

"That was excellent, Libby. I thank you."

"It is rare that I have a guest, John. The pleasure was mine."

"Not yet," he said with a smile.

"I was hoping you would be able to stay the night."

He took his time looking her over, from her barely concealed bosom to the loveliness of her face, framed by that mass of shining black hair. "I'm not sure that even Lem could keep me from it," he said.

"Now that, sir, is a compliment."

"It was intended as one. Would you, uh, mind if we sit and talk for a little while before we go upstairs?"

"I would prefer it." She rose gracefully from her chair at the head of the table. "Brandy?"

"Please."

"We will have coffee and brandy in the parlor, Elsie," she said to the serving girl who was hovering near the kitchen door. Lem, Slocum was sure, would be nearby also.

Libby led the way to the parlor and lowered herself into a chair. The coffee and brandy were served within seconds after she was seated, and Elsie left the room.

"Was there something in particular on your mind, John?"

"Other than you, you mean?" he teased. "Is that possible?"

"You are a flatterer, sir, and I enjoy that. But I suspect there is more to life than dalliance." She smiled. "Is that really true?"

"Barely," he said.

"In any event, you seem a bit preoccupied. What was it you wanted to say?"

"Ask, not say. I was curious about the feud between the Calders and the, uh, folks I met the night you found me."

A look of distaste flashed across Libby's pretty features.

"Did I bring up a painful subject?"

"Yes," she admitted.

"I'm sorry, I—"

"No, it's all right. At least to the extent that you are not responsible for any of it. And truly I do not mind telling you our side of it."

Slocum nodded and waited, enjoying a sip of the excellent brandy that had been served. The mellow richness of it suggested that the brandy might have been part of a stock laid in when times were better at The Oaks.

"It probably would be more ladylike for me to say nothing," Libby said. "You know. If you cannot say something pleasant about a person, say nothing at all. That sort of thing."

Slocum nodded again and continued to wait. It was apparent that she wanted to speak but was having to work herself into it.

"Conjecture is particularly inappropriate, I have been taught, John, and guesswork is most of what we know about the Calders' circumstances. In fairness I should also say that perception may be colored by prejudice.

Which is possible in this case. Also, as you may well recall, emotions ran rather high during the recent war. Logic is not always a survivor when the emotions are intense."

"You've apologized pretty thoroughly," Slocum said. "Now go ahead and tell me what you think."

Libby sat looking not at Slocum but across the room and far beyond, her eyes unfocused and distant as she assembled her thoughts.

"Back during the war," she began, "there were very few in this area who offered less than wholehearted support for the cause of the Confederacy. No one would have dreamt of actually supporting the Union, but there were a few who declined to . . . participate . . . themselves . . . in the cause."

She hesitated.

"Warren Calder was one of those?" Slocum suggested for her.

She looked his way and gave him a small, grateful smile. "By our standards and depth of conviction . . . yes."

"Um," Slocum said noncommittally. He wanted her to take it as encouragement to continue, and she did.

"While others donned the butternut and went forth to fight, Mr. Calder was among those who remained behind. Later, when the nation was in such critical need of foodstuffs to provide for our gallant young men, Mr. Calder was among those who agreed to furnish some of the necessaries." Again she paused. Slocum waited her out.

"It was said—mind you, John, I do not know this as certain knowledge, but the talk sprang from the buyers themselves and not from the community, or I should not repeat it even now—but it was said that when finally he agreed to furnish beef for the Army, Warren Calder demanded his payment in gold coin. It is said that he was never known to accept nor to pass paper money of the Confederacy."

That, Slocum knew, would be indictment enough to

damn a man anywhere in the South. Confederate paper had been without value virtually from the beginning of the conflict, but the people who supported the cause accepted the paper at face value as an expression of their love for the fledgling and so short-lived nation it had represented.

"Moreover," Libby went on, "there were suspicions that arose because Mr. Calder delivered beef to the Army yet seemed to have no lack of more beef to deliver whenever more gold coin was available for payment."

Slocum's eyebrows went up.

"What I am . . . oh, I simply know no delicate way to put this, John."

"It's all right, Libby. I'm only listening; I'm not judging either you or Calder."

"Very well, then." She sighed. "You see, John, before the war, there were some of us who had been here for thirty years or more, since back when the territory became part of the Union. Those of us who had been established here for some time had rather sizable herds of cattle on the land, mostly Cuban stock brought in by way of Fort Brooke. Our families had fought Indians and climate and disease. And we prevailed. By the time of the outbreak of hostilities with those damnable mechanics, our herds were well established if not yet flourishing.

"Yet during the war, when our men were off in Virginia and Mississippi and the Good Lord knows wherever else, those herds dwindled at a terrible rate. To the point where few of us have anything of value left. Certainly I do not.

"And a few miles away, Warren Calder, who was able to sell beef to the commissary buyers on frequent occasion, well, suffice it to say that *his* herds prospered and grew through those selfsame years of difficulty. Now he is the only large-scale rancher remaining between the Hillsborough and the Kissimmee rivers. The *only* one."

Slocum grunted. "The sonuvabitch is a rustler, huh?"

"I beg your pardon?"

"Sorry. It's an expression used back where I generally do my wandering. A cow thief in plainer language. And a sonuvabitch either side of the big river."

"Much of what I said is guesswork, John. You must remember that."

"Oh, I do, Libby. I promised you that." Slocum grinned. "But you gotta remember, I was wearin' one of those gray uniforms too. And there was times when I was as hungry and cold and wet as any of the boys that marched off from this part of the country. I don't reckon I could work up a whole hell of a lot of sympathy for a profiteer."

Libby sighed. "Nor could we. And now we are finding it impossible to rebuild. Our stock still do poorly, and our grazing land is severely limited. Everywhere one of us tries to establish cattle, there are Calder herds already there to use the little grass that is available. The land is theoretically open for all to use, but it seems more and more that might equates to right, particularly the right to use public grazing lands. Some have begun trying to fight back the only way they know how. But I think that cause is as doomed to failure as was the Confederacy, John. We simply haven't the strength to hold on much longer." She looked wistfully around her at the lovely room where they sat. "I suspect that eventually I shall be forced to give up The Oaks. I will regret that. Truly I shall."

Slocum reached forward from his chair. He took her hand and gave it a gentle squeeze. "I hope you're wrong about that. It's pretty easy to see that you love it."

"My family is gone. The Oaks is all I have left of them. The tie I have with it is much stronger than to a house and a piece of land. It is all I have."

"At least," Slocum said, "you aren't giving up."

"Never."

He nodded and sighed. Taking her hand again, he

stood and drew her to her feet. "Shall we retire now, milady?"

Libby smiled. "With a much greater pleasure, sir, than our conversation has given." She led the way toward the stairs.

31

Slocum sat up and wiped his chin with a lewd wink and a grin. "Is the service acceptable, ma'am?"

"I have never been serviced better," Libby said contentedly.

Damned if she didn't sound like she meant it, too, Slocum thought. He lay down beside her and held her close. The truth was, he felt rather good himself, although his usual style was to take before he gave.

There was something about this woman, though, that made a man want to be more than he was. For her.

The contrast between Elizabeth Ashford and Rose Calder was startling. The contrast between his feelings when he was with one of them was even more extreme.

With Rose he wanted to rip and tear. He wanted to rip her gash apart with the power of his cock. He did not want to make love with her, he wanted to rape her. Time and time again.

But with Libby he felt like . . . a gentleman.

The thought astonished him. A gentleman? John Slocum? He shook his head. It had been a long, long time since anyone had perceived John Slocum as a gentleman. And then it had taken an act of the Confederate Congress to accomplish that monumental task.

Now it seemed that the lightest touch of Libby Ashford's fingers on his wrist could accomplish as much.

No, he decided. More. Because this time *he* almost believed it himself.

He pulled her closer and felt her nuzzle into the hollow of his shoulder.

"What are you thinking?" she asked softly.

He smiled. "What a truly marvelous woman you are, Libby Ashford."

She sighed. "I've waited all my life to meet a man like you, John Slocum." She raised her head and looked at him. "You know, John, I think you are man enough to stand against anything. I think you could even keep The Oaks for me if I could convince you to become a part of it."

Slocum felt a sharp pang deep in his gut. "Jesus, woman, don't do that."

"What?"

"Don't go to reading my damn mind like that."

"Really?"

Reluctantly he nodded. "I'm not a man to settle down, Libby. Not anyplace. But the pull is stronger with you than . . . than I would ever have believed possible. You're that much woman, lady. And that is one hell of a lot of woman."

"Have you ever tried it?"

He shrugged. "Once upon a time. Sort of."

"But never with me," she said huskily. The soft sound of her voice—and her meaning—sent a wave of mingled joy and fear through Slocum's veins.

"I don't know, Libby. This country down here . . . it's so damned *different*. It's hardly my idea of paradise." He sighed. "But I admit that maybe you are. Shit!" He turned away from her.

"I have little to offer, John, other than myself. But I believe, sir, that I have fallen irrevocably in love with you."

Slocum clamped his mouth shut. There was an easy response to that. Too easy. And there are some things that a man does not say when they come too easily.

"This wild country where you live, John. Have you considered how a genteel but destitute Florida belle might fit into it beside you?"

"Yeah," he said curtly. "Considered it."

"And?"

A flash of anger shoved him into a sitting position,

and he snapped at her, "Goddamn it, woman, you don't know me. You don't know shit about me. I've killed men. I'm a gunfighter, not some gentleman soldier. There's no fucking glory out there. There's blood and dust and hard times. I've robbed banks and worse. There's wanted posters on me in half the states and territories the other side of the Mississippi. Maybe more'n half. And that's just a tiny bit of the things you don't know about me. Jesus, woman. Get serious, will you?"

"I suggest, sir," she said softly, "that there are things about me that you do not suspect also. For instance, I do not care what you have been. Nor even what you might become. I would be proud to be your woman regardless."

Slocum groaned. "You're wrong, Libby. I did suspect that about you. It's just one of the things I admire about you. But I've considered something else, too. If I took you away from The Oaks, you'd hate me inside a month for having done it. This place, your heritage more than the place that represents it, why, that's so much a part of you that you couldn't help but learn to hate me if I took you away from it. Hell, I wouldn't even blame you."

Libby reached up and stroked his face. She slid a finger between his lips and toyed with his tongue. "The fact remains, John Slocum, I love you. You may have me on any terms you care to name. Here or anywhere. Tonight or forever. Whatever brings you pleasure."

She sat up and gave him a bright if rather forced smile. "And now, sir, please do me the kindness to lie down. I believe that marvelous cock of yours requires draining." She laughed, genuinely this time. "Besides, it seems I may be in a competition with Rose Calder, according to what the servants tell me. And the young lady does have the advantage of years on me. If I want to keep your lovely pecker out of her overly broad ass, I really must be willing to demonstrate that mine is superior."

"Overly broad?" Slocum asked with a grin. "Is that jealousy talking?"

"I think not."

Slocum just grinned. Actually, Rose's ass was formed rather nicely. It was only the extravagantly tiny size of her waist that might make her seem broad in the beam. And then only when she was dressed.

But this was hardly the time to argue about another woman's anatomy.

Slocum lay back on the canopied bed and allowed Libby Ashford to prove her own desirability as a superior cocksucker and superb piece of elegant ass.

Damned if she wasn't able to do it, too.

32

Slocum slipped the bridle over the ears of the Calder pony and turned it loose in the corral with a slap on its scrawny rump. He slung the saddle over his shoulder and humped it toward the shed.

After the bright Florida sunshine, the interior of the shed seemed as black as midnight, and he stopped in the doorway to let his eyes adjust before he went any further.

He heard a noise, a faint rustling and no more, from inside the shed. It might have been nothing more harmful than a rat, but John Slocum had not survived as long as he had by making assumptions. He let the saddle and bridle fall to the ground unheeded and threw himself sideways as soon as his always keenly tuned ears received that hint of sound. If it was a rat, he could pick them up and brush them off and no harm would have been done.

But it was not some prowling rodent.

No sooner had Slocum vacated the doorway than the lash of a bullwhip licked nastily into the opening, its cracker snapping with pistol-shot abruptness.

That cracker would have sliced knife-clean through cloth and flesh had Slocum not moved.

With a roar Slocum charged forward into the shadowy interior of the shed. The horse pistol he had in his belt carried only one shot, and he as yet could not see well enough to know where to aim. And he knew that there are only two defenses against a whip. The first is to run like hell. The second is to get inside the effective range of the whip and beat the shit out of the man using it. Slocum chose the latter.

His shoulder smashed into someone and sent him sprawling. A few paces to the left Slocum could hear someone else's feet moving. There were two of them at least, then.

With one down, if only for the moment, he flung himself in the direction of the second.

His eyes were adjusting now, and he could see the pale blur of a man's face. This was no time for the pleasantries of boxing rules. Slocum thrust his extended fingers into the man's eyes and was rewarded with a high-pitched scream. He stayed with that one long enough to plant a knee into the bastard's crotch and then whirled to face the other.

That man—it was one of Calder's cowboys, he could see now—was just regaining his feet. There was an uncoiled whip lying in the dirt floor at his feet.

Before he could get himself set, Slocum stepped forward and drove the toe of his boot into the bridge of the man's nose, collapsing him without a whimper.

Outside, though, there was the sound of running feet.

Jesus, Slocum thought. The whole fucking crew.

The cracker with the crushed balls stirred on the ground behind Slocum. If he was going to have to fight all of them there seemed no point in allowing second chances. Slocum turned and kicked the man in the side of the head. The fellow quit moving and lay still after that.

Slocum pulled out the big horse pistol as the rest of them reached the doorway, but another of those ever present blacksnake whips flickered and the pistol went flying. Slocum was lucky to have kept his fingers.

The crackers spilled through the door and jammed the interior of the saddle shed. They were deathly silent and intent on the business of destroying him. The only good thing about there being so damned many of them was that there was no room for them to bring their fucking whips into play. If they forced him outside, though, they would be able to cut him into hors d'oeuvre size pieces. He put his back to the corner and let them come.

Honus Luther was in the lead. Slocum dropped him with another well-aimed kick to the cods and a chop to the throat.

There were more behind Luther, though. Too many more. They swarmed onto and over him.

Slocum kicked and punched and bit whatever and whenever he could, but there were just too many of them. They overwhelmed him and pummeled him viciously to the ground. He was aswim in a sea of pounding fists and sweaty armpits and long unwashed butts. They slammed him into the dirt and punched and kicked at him, getting in their own way when one or two of them could have done serious if not lethal damage. Slocum curled into a tight ball and tried to protect his vital organs as well as he could.

Finally someone hauled them apart—or maybe they simply got tired from so much punching and kicking—and the crowd thinned around him.

"Pick him up an' get him out t' the corral," someone said. Slocum thought it was Luther's voice. He thought it would be a good idea to remember that little fact.

Hands, a good many hands, grabbed him and hauled him to his feet. The crackers were still wary of Slocum's strength. They pinned his arms to his sides as they hustled him out the door.

"That's a good one over there. Plenty tall. Tie him to it."

Slocum was flung face forward into a tall corral post. Willing hands reached around him to wrap him with stout rope and tie him against the post.

Other hands pulled at his arms and forced his hands out away from his body. His wrists were lashed to the top rail of the corral, where a few days before the crackers had sat hoping to watch Honus Luther beat him. More hands yanked his legs wide and tied his knees to lower rails.

Within seconds he was immobile, spread-eagled and unable to move.

Slocum clenched his teeth and applied all of his

massive strength against the ropes that were restraining him. Fury had consumed him, and he wanted nothing but to break the ropes and charge barehanded into the cowardly pack of crackers who had mobbed him.

He wanted to bring them thunder and lightning and a rain of death.

But the ropes were too strong, the knots too well tied. He strained until blood ran at his wrists from the grating of hemp on flesh, and he was unable to break the bonds.

He turned to look at them, and deep within his eyes an icy green fire flashed and burned.

Several of the cowboys stumbled backward at the sight of his naked fury, and others turned their eyes away unable to look into John Slocum's face.

There was not a man among them who could have faced him alone and had the courage to stand there.

But they were not alone. And Slocum was not free to throw himself against them. He was tied and helpless, and that knowledge gave them a false courage that even liquor could not have accomplished.

"Strip the bastard's shirt off, boys," the voice called again. Slocum was sure this time that it was Honus Luther. Slocum would remember. His will to survive intensified. He wanted nothing more than to survive whatever was to come. So that he could kill Honus Luther and as many more of them as he could manage. If nothing else, he wanted to do that. And if he died two seconds afterward, he wouldn't care. Just so he could take Luther down with John Slocum's hands wrapped around Luther's throat until face turned purple and his tongue protruded through lifeless blue lips.

The hands grabbed his shirt at the collar and yanked down and sideways. Cloth tore, and Slocum could feel the beat of the sun against his back and a light movement of hot air.

"Gimme that blacksnake," Luther said.

Slocum was not surprised. He had guessed what was to come as soon as they had tied him. He raged again against the ropes that held him but with no more success than he had found before. His lips drew back from his teeth in a snarl of rage.

"Perfect," Luther said.

Slocum could sense the men parting behind his back, clearing a path for Honus Luther's whip. He braced himself.

"Somebody count 'em out for me, boys," Luther said. "I wanta see just how many it takes to finish this son of a fucking bitch."

Slocum tensed.

Even so, he was unable to stop the hiss of breath being driven from his body when the fire of the lash tip bit deep into the unprotected skin and muscle of his back. It was worse, far worse, than falling onto a bed of white-hot coals.

He was not, he was *not* going to give them the satisfaction of hearing him cry out. He clenched his teeth together until his neck corded and the tendons stood out stark and plain at the sides of his jaw. He would *not* give those bastards any satisfaction.

"One," a voice counted aloud.

33

The voice Slocum was expecting would have called out "seven" to keep Honus Luther's count.

Instead there was an angry shout and the sound of approaching hoofbeats.

Slocum managed to raise his head and turn it enough to see that Boyd Calder was riding up on a reasonably handsome gray horse that Slocum did not remember seeing around the place before.

"What the hell is going on here?" the kid demanded before he reached a halt. He sprang out of the saddle and threw his reins to the nearest cowboy. "Cut him loose. *Now*, goddamnit! Luther, you get your ass off this ranch. If you set foot on it again, I'll have you shot where you're seen. The rest of you. Do you hear that? Any sonuvabitch that sees Honus Luther anywhere on this ranch better either shoot him or pack his gear the hell off of it too, because you'll be on the list next."

"No," Slocum said. It came out more croak than word. "No," he repeated. He licked dry lips and swallowed. "You keep him around, Boyd. I want to have a word with him. Just me an' him."

One of the crackers was already engaged in cutting Slocum's hands free, and Slocum got a look at Honus Luther's face when Slocum turned to look him in the eye. The man became suddenly pale.

"You—you'll thank me when you hear the whole of it, Boyd," Luther stammered. "I swear to God you will."

The kid looked damn well skeptical. "Well?" he demanded. "I didn't tell you to quit cuttin' on John's ropes. You turn him loose like I said. Well, Luther, are you gonna talk or are you gonna run?'' He took a look toward Slocum. ''Frankly, if I was you I'd grab a fast horse and start in runnin'.''

''Don't let that sonuvabitch get away,'' Luther told the other crackers with another frightened look toward Slocum. ''Don't let him do nothing.''

''I'm not going anywhere,'' Slocum assured him. ''Not unless you try to. Besides which, I want to hear this my own self. Nobody's yet got around to telling me why I was jumped.''

''We're waiting,'' Boyd reminded.

''Yeah, well, the thing is,'' Luther said nervously, ''the thing is, I was watchin' the Ashford place like I was told. Your daddy tol' me to do that, you know. I was over there on his orders.''

''So?''

''So what I seen was this Slocum prick sneakin' in the front door just as sassy as any o' them squatters that your daddy has got such a hard-on about. Went in as cool as you please and spent damn-all amount o' time with that stuck-up bitch Elizabeth Ashford.'' He glared at Slocum, regaining confidence now that he was talking and not having to run. ''You know as good as your daddy does, Boyd, that there's no Calder hand has any business around that Ashford place nor any of them squatter places. An' while I was over there watchin' it came to me that all we got is this fucker's word that he was jumped and near hung by that crowd. Nothin' but his word on it. Personally, as far as I'm concerned, his word don't count for shit when I can see with my own eyes that he's sucking up to the squatters. Why, we none of us ever seen him nor heard of him till we run into him that day on the road. Shit, Boyd, he could be a spy for them squatters right from the word go. Coulda been sent in here deliberate to find out what we're up to and reportin' to 'em through the Ashford bitch right along. You think about that, Boyd. Just think on it.''

Luther was looking self-righteous and confident again

now. He folded his arms and stared Slocum in the eyes for the first time since Slocum had been cut free.

"Is Luther telling the truth, John? Were you really at The Oaks like he says?"

Slocum grunted. He made the mistake of leaning back against the corral rails, and a jolt of intense pain straightened him up again when the gashes on his back contacted the rough wood of the poles.

"I was there, all right. You gave me some time to rest up, and I spent it over there. As for spying, shit, I wouldn't know anything to tell them if I wanted to. Which I ain't got no reason for doing to begin with."

"But you were there? Dammit, John, that's the enemy camp. Whatever would take you over to The Oaks?"

"Come off it, Boyd. There's not but one reason for me to go over there, and you know it."

"To tell them what you seen here," Luther shouted.

There was a murmur of anger from the other men as well. It took no special genius to know where they stood.

"No, I don't know, John. Not unless Luther is right about you. Which I admit I can't hardly believe. I mean, shit, you and me have been friends, John. I can't believe you'd turn on me like this."

Slocum snorted his disgust. It was apparent that Honus Luther's conviction was beginning to sway Boyd's judgment. If nothing else, it had created the first stirrings of doubt in the boy's mind.

"Jesus, Boyd, I went over and spent two nights in that house because Libby Ashford is one hell of a fine-looking woman, and I was getting horny. *Now* do you understand?"

Admitting that was one hell of an ungentlemanly thing to do, but it was the only excuse other than Luther's that Slocum could think of to take him to The Oaks. His admission had nothing to do with the fact that it happened to be the truth. It was simply the only reason he could think of that might be accepted as logical and reasonable by the irate crackers. Including Boyd Calder.

"Do you mean . . . oh." Boyd at least had the good grace to look embarrassed. "Well, Honus?"

"You ain't gonna believe a bullshit story like that, are you, Boyd? Can you imagine Miss High An' Mighty Ashford liftin' her dress for *him*? Or for anybody else fer that matter?"

"I'd damn sure like to see her lift it fer *me*," a voice came from the crowd.

Several of the men chuckled and nodded their heads in agreement, and some of the tension seemed to drain from the group.

"I'll tell you what, Luther," Slocum said. "Why don't you come over here an' get down on your knees. I'll let you smell of my pecker real close up. I hear you like to do that sort of thing anyway. Then you can tell all of us if you think it's been used lately."

Luther turned such a violent shade of red that Slocum began to wonder if he had accidentally struck a nerve and the guy *was* limp-wristed when no one was looking.

Luther sputtered angrily, but he couldn't get any words to come out.

"Look, Boyd," Slocum said, "I don't intend to go any further with this horseshit. You're okay, rooster, but the rest of this sad-assed collection of cracker cowboys smells too ripe for me to want to be around them anymore. What I wanted here—and you offered it without me ever thinking of asking—was a job that would get me back to Texas where I belong. As far as I'm concerned, you can damn well pay me off. I'll have my little conversation with ol' Honus here and be on my way."

Luther became pale again. He seemed to have forgotten that someone was going to have to make amends for what had been done to John Slocum. And now that Slocum was free and still alive, it looked like Honus Luther had been elected to provide payment in full.

"Don't let him go nowhere," Luther cried. "My God, boys, string him up. Do something. Don't just turn him loose, for God's sake."

Slocum grinned at him. "For God's sake, Honus? Or for yours? Ah well, you can sort that out later. After all, you'll be seeing Him soon enough."

Luther seemed to sag at the knees. He turned to Boyd. "Please, Boyd. Don't just turn him loose. *Don't* do that."

The kid glanced from Luther to Slocum and back again. "You know, Honus," he said reflectively, "you put some bad marks on John's back. I expect we'll want to fix him up as best we can, and pay him what we owe him, and give him a bait of feed. He might even want to spend the night. But he's a free man. I can't hold him from doing what he wants. If I was you, Honus, I think I would give some real strong thought to getting the hell out of here while I still could."

Luther was trembling so hard now that his shakes were clearly visible to those around him.

Slocum, watching him, sidled close to one of the cowboys who had cut him loose. He measured the distance from his hand to the cracker's belt and waited.

With a scream that was more fear than anything else, Honus Luther grabbed for the pistol he was carrying in his waistband.

Slocum was ready for him. His hand flashed to the cowboy's belt, swept the cracker's knife from its sheath, and before Luther could get a shot off, the borrowed knife was buried hilt deep in the hollow of his throat, his blood pumping out into the sand.

The rest of them, Boyd included, stood in shocked silence. Apparently, none of these boys were used to the idea of unannounced violence.

"Poor bastard was just too scared to run, I reckon," Slocum observed. He shrugged. "Say, Petey? Thanks for the loan of your knife."

He turned and walked toward the house, careful to allow no letdown that would show a single one of those pricks how badly they had hurt him. He wouldn't give them that or any other kind of satisfaction. Not as long as he could draw breath.

34

Warren Calder did not seem a whole hell of a lot happier with him than Honus Luther had been, back when Honus Luther was alive, but the man kept his mouth shut about it. Mrs. Calder did not seem to give much of a shit about anything, Slocum thought. Still, he gave in to Boyd's insistence that he stay overnight. He wouldn't have done that except that his back felt like it was still being bathed in torch flames every time he moved. They had to bring a stool to the table for him to sit on while he ate because he couldn't stand the back of a chair behind him.

Afterward, with some of Warren Calder's gold coins in his pocket, Slocum allowed Rose to apply a coat of grease to the gashes sliced into the meat of his back.

She did it with surprising tenderness and concern for his welfare, which was much more than he would have expected from her after the last time they had spent together.

"Tonight, John," she whispered while her parents and brother were on the far side of the room, "we'll have to be very careful of your poor back. I'll be very gentle with you. Or if it'll make you feel better you can rough me up again."

Slocum looked at her with amazement in his eyes. Rose really seemed to have enjoyed his brutal treatment of her as much as he had. She was even asking for more of the same.

And with her, the way he reacted to her, he was not at all sure that he would not give her more of the same again.

Yet, looking at her, he could not help wanting her.

Even knowing that Libby Ashford was only a matter of miles away, knowing that Libby could satisfy any man's dreams, he still wanted Rose Calder, too. And if he was going to spend the night under this roof, he was going to spend it in Rose's bed. If he was a gentleman, he thought, he probably should be feeling some sense of shame about that. Which was proof enough that he was no gentleman. All he was feeling about the prospect was an erection.

"I'll let you know later," he whispered.

Rose and her mother went off to some other part of the ugly, sprawling house soon after Slocum's back had been treated, and Warren Calder disappeared soon after them. Boyd brought Slocum a drink and sneaked one for himself; his mother did not like for him to drink, but if Slocum did he would also.

"Thanks, rooster. That's just what I needed."

"I really think you oughta stay, John," the boy said for perhaps the thousandth time. "The sheriff might wanta ask you some questions or something."

Slocum grinned. "Hell, rooster, that's the best reason I've heard yet for me to leave. I got troubles enough without adding more of that kind."

"Aw, he wouldn't bother you. It was self-defense, clear enough. We all seen it."

"True. So there's no point in making a big deal out of it, right?"

"Whatever you say, John. But I'm gonna miss you. I mean, how often do I get to meet a real westerner down here."

Slocum shrugged but wished he had not as soon as the pain hit him from the movement. The grease had helped but not all that much. "Come out to where the country's big and open then, rooster. You'd damn sure like it."

"Oh, I know that, John. Don't I just know it. But Pa needs me here now. Needs you too for that matter. We got to have all the hands we can get." He smiled. "Come to think of it, you already done took one of our hands away. The least you can do is to replace him for as long as we need.''

"Come on, Boyd, I done your daddy a favor by reducing his payroll for him. You already got half again as many cowboys as you could ever hope to need for the amount of cows you own and five years increase besides. I mean, I ain't entirely stupid when it comes to cattle, rooster. And I know something about fighting, too. You outnumber the other side at least two to one, and it might be more than that. You don't need any more hands, you need less. Be better off all the way around.''

"No, you don't understand. We really do need more. As many as we can get hold of.''

"What the hell for?'' Slocum took a drink from the glass Boyd had given him. He had no idea what the stuff was except that it could not begin to compare with the fine brandy Libby Ashford had served him. Still, it was liquor and a painkiller and it was definitely better than a kick in the teeth. He took another swallow. "Cat got your tongue, rooster?''

"No, it's just that, well, we ain't supposed to talk about it.''

"Oh.'' Slocum took another drink. It tasted better after the initial knock. Half a dozen or so and it might actually start to taste good.

Slocum would have been willing to let the matter drop there. After all, he cared damned little about the Calder affairs at this point and was more than willing to let them keep their secrets. But Boyd continued.

"Listen, John, if I tell you, will you stay? Please?'' He looked as eager and hopeful as a pup sitting beside the dinner table.

Slocum smiled at him. "Prob'ly not, rooster. I won't make you no promises that I'm not willing to keep.''

"Will you *think* about it? Will you at least do that?''

"Hell, kid, I'll think about damn near any scheme you tell me. But I won't make you promises. And more'n likely I'll be riding out of here tomorrow morning just like I told you I was going to do. Is that fair?''

"That's fair, John. That's more than fair. But I am gonna ask you to hear me out and at least do some thinking about helping. We need all the help we can get to resolve this range war with the squatters, and you could sure enough help us, John. You sure could.''

The kid took a hurried gulp of his drink, and Slocum had to smile at watching Boyd choke and try to hide it.

Then Boyd began to talk. It took him only a few moments to explain. It was very simple.

The question then was, What was Slocum going to do about it?

35

Slocum hobbled to the door to answer the knock. Now that no one was there to see, he had been letting himself go, giving in to the pain the whipping had caused. His major regret about that experience now was that Honus Luther had died too damn easily. Given any choice at all, Slocum would have preferred to get the man off to himself and apply some none too delicate tricks he had seen as Kiowa handiwork.

Bastard, he thought again. But when he reached the door and pulled it open he was standing straight and tall, and there was no hint of pain on his face.

"Damn," he said. "I thought I was supposed to slink around to your room, Rose."

"Your back must be hurting you, so I thought this would be easier. Besides, I wasn't sure that you would come to me. I . . . understand you've been over to Elizabeth Ashford's home for the past few days. And nights."

Slocum could not restrain a grin. There was something to be said for the idea of having several women anxious to compete with one another for his masculine favors. Quite a lot to be said for it, actually. He stepped back and let Rose into the room.

The girl pressed her hands against his chest, careful not to reach around and risk touching the open wounds on his back. She let her robe fall from her shoulders and rubbed her large, proud breasts across his chest.

She took his hand and lifted it to cup one of those impressive tits. "Elizabeth Ashford doesn't have anything like this, John," she whispered. "Squeeze it."

He did. "Harder. I don't care if you hurt me. Squeeze it. Try to tear it off if you want. I won't mind."

Slocum groaned and grabbed her to him. He jammed his tongue between her teeth and she opened her mouth to him. She had a musky, dark flavor to her that excited him and made him want to ravish her, and it was obvious from the way she rubbed her pudendum against him, grinding herself against his leg, that she was every bit as excited as he.

Her arms wrapped around him, and in spite of himself Slocum winced and pulled away from her with the onslaught of pain.

"Oh, John, I'm so sorry. Please, please forgive me." Incredibly, she began to cry at the idea of having hurt him. He was touched by her tears.

"Hey, it's all right. Really. But, uh, to be honest, I'd rather you didn't do it again."

"I won't. I swear I won't."

He wiped her tears away with the balls of his thumbs and said, "Listen, I think we might be more comfortable over on that bed."

She nodded and moved to the side of the bed to stand and wait for him. Slocum held back for a moment, pausing to savor the sight of her as she stood naked and eager for him to join her.

Her body was beautiful, he had to admit. He found himself comparing Rose's lush, ripe figure to Libby's slender, taut form, and he discovered that he would not have been able to choose between them. Each woman had so much to offer. And each was so willing to give it without reservation or claim upon him.

He grinned. Shee-it, he thought, not quite *every* damn thing about this humid hellhole of a country was really so awful.

He crossed the room to stand in front of her, and once again that fierce, overwhelming desire to master her possessed him. He grasped her roughly under the chin and forced her head back, yanking her to him and descending upon her waiting mouth with an assault that was more an oral ravishment than a kiss.

He took hold of her breast and squeezed harshly, knowing he was hurting her, knowing that she welcomed the pain he gave her.

"Ahhhhh," she moaned. She found his free hand and raised it to her other breast, and he pulped her tender flesh between powerful fingers.

Even knowing her as he had come to, he was amazed when he felt Rose shudder and vibrate with the internal explosions of a powerful climax as he clutched her.

She pulled her mouth away from his and stroked the side of his neck lovingly. "Thank you, John," she breathed.

With this wild woman Slocum felt no tenderness whatsoever, though. He released his hold on her breasts and took her by the shoulders hard enough to leave a bruise. He shoved her to her knees and took a handful of honey-colored hair, jamming her face onto him and forcing himself deep into her.

She bent herself to his desires compliantly, pulling hard against him and making low, crooning, gobbling sounds as she serviced him.

"Get up," he said harshly. Still keeping his hold in her hair he pulled her to her feet and threw her onto the bed. She lay where she fell, sprawled and waiting, eager now to please him.

Slocum looked down at her. Her body was glorious, and he was its master. For the first time he had a sense of what it had been to own another human being.

He stalked around to the far side of the bed and bent over her, pulling her roughly to and slightly beyond the side of the bed so that her head hung down.

He bent and again entered her throat, ramming himself full length into her until he came close to an explosion. And then quickly he backed off. Not yet. He wanted to prolong this. He wanted to enjoy all of it that there was for him to take.

"Are you all right?"

He nodded.

"Let me. Please."

She guided him, drawing him gently down onto the bed so that he lay partially on the mattress but with his legs extended and braced on the floor. His massive tool hung free, pointing toward the floor.

Rose slipped off the bed and lowered herself to the floor between his feet. She lay on her back and pulled herself forward until she was half sitting, half leaning against the side of the bed. She raised her lips to him and at the same time had both hands free to fondle his balls and tickle that sensitive area between scrotum and anus. The combination of sensations was enough to give a city man heart failure. Slocum was not sure he himself would not be driven out of his mind before she finished.

"Wait, dammit," he ordered. "Not yet."

Obediently she stopped. She released him and waited where she was.

"Turn around," he ordered.

"What?"

"Here."

He guided her, moving Rose so that she was braced with her back on the floor and her soft, pinkly glowing ass propped high against the side of the bed, much like a headstand gone awry with her legs positioned down by her shoulders. The maneuver left her pussy exposed to him, high and spread wide. He could see droplets of hot juices flowing, to the extent that her pubic hair was damp and matted.

"That's good," Slocum said.

He poised himself over her and let his huge cock slide deeper and ever deeper into her.

The angle gave him more access to her body than he had ever had before, and she cried out softly as the incredible stallion length of him filled her and stretched her beyond anything she might have imagined possible. She had taken all of him before, she had thought, but never anything like this. Pain and pleasure flooded through her at the same time, and she reached up to titillate her own hard clitoris while Slocum stroked in and out of her aching body.

Slocum could feel what she was doing, and he pumped into her harder and faster, driving himself upon her with as much anger as desire.

Once again he found himself wanting to rip her apart, and he drove himself into her with a frenzy of motion.

He felt her shudder and knew that she had come, and he savaged her with his cock. He felt the pounding head of his tool smash into the upper reaches of her hole and he rammed himself forward harder and harder against that blockage, trying to batter his way into her gut, trying to jam it so deep it would come out through her throat from below.

He felt her shake and quiver beneath his pounding and knew that he was hurting her. He thought that he felt a tearing of tender flesh, and that was enough to send him careening over the edge into a volcano explosion of boiling cum.

Rose cried out beneath him, and he was satisfied. When he withdrew from her and stood tall and powerful over her there was a smear of blood on his pecker and at the gaping, wet, well-used lips of the woman's sex.

Her eyes were closed, and he wondered for a moment if she was unconscious, but her lids fluttered and she opened her eyes to look adoringly up at him.

"Again? Please?"

He nodded his permission and Rose came to her knees to clean him with her tongue and to begin anew.

Slocum closed his eyes and let this woman tend to him. She was wilder, perhaps, than any female he had ever known. Yet in a way, his own dark desires when he was with her disturbed him, and he knew that he would be glad to leave this house come morning.

36

"I want to tell you, rooster, I appreciate all you've done for me," Slocum said as he pulled the hackamore over the ears of the pony and adjusted it to hang correctly.

The kid looked embarrassed and hung his head.

The truth was that he had done a good deal to help Slocum on his way, and Slocum knew it. Boyd had given him a horse to ride. Well, a horse of sorts. It was an undersized little thing even by the Florida swamp standards and was so poorly made as to be ludicrous. It probably was not worth five dollars. It was also a damn sight better than walking.

The kid had also given him his pick—Slocum suspected without Warren Calder's knowledge—from the chest of elderly revolvers, so once again there was a .36 Navy in Slocum's belt. He had been able to choose among Colts, Griswold and Griers, Dance Brothers, even a Starr they had found somewhere. But the well-balanced Navy was the best among them, and Slocum had not hesitated in his choosing.

A saddle and bridle had seemed a bit much, apparently, and Boyd had not offered those, but Slocum required only a few minutes to fashion a hackamore out of some scraps of rawhide and lengths of twine. Slocum had ridden bareback more than a few times before, and if the ugly little horse was halfway sane, Slocum would have no problems getting from here to there.

"If you ever do decide to come west, kid," Slocum said as he finished his adjustments, "well, I can't tell you where to look me up 'cause I never know from one day to the next where the wind's likely to carry me. But if I ever run into you, I'd be proud to tell you howdy.

And that ain't something I say to just any man." Slocum turned and held his hand out.

Boyd looked as grateful as he was unhappy about this western man's leave-taking, and he reached out.

Before they could shake, though, there was a sound of footsteps and Warren Calder came into view.

"What's this?" the old man demanded.

"I said good-bye once already," Slocum told him. "That's always seemed enough to me before."

"No, goddamnit, how are you fixing to ride out on one of my horses?"

Slocum glared at him and tossed him the bridle he had made from a cast-off piece of rope. "Reckon I'm not, then."

The old bastard was pushing him, and Slocum did not take to being pushed. Even if he did owe the old prick a debt of sorts for his son's hospitality.

Still, after what Libby had told him, and after what Boyd himself had outlined the night before, Slocum was more than a little tired of Warren Calder himself. The attitude of the man's cracker cowboys and the stinking country he lived in were just so much icing on a cake of dislike.

"Wait, Pa, I gave John that pony. It's mine, or it was till I decided to give it away."

"And that gun in his belt?" Calder said, pointing.

"Dammit, Pa, if I can't do some little thing without asking your permission every time I turn around, why, I reckon I might just walk along with John for as far as he's going." Boyd was looking angry now.

"You wouldn't have the nerve to—"

"Quit, the both of you," Slocum interrupted. They did. "Sometime, Warren, you ought to take a look at this boy of yours. You might like what you saw if you ever paid any attention to him. He's all right. Better'n you deserve, as a matter of fact. I'd tell you more 'cept I like rooster too much to want him to hear all that I'd say."

Calder did not like that, but he did not argue. Slocum

would have welcomed any excuse to tear into the carpetbagging sonuvabitch, and Calder might well have seen that in Slocum's expression. For whatever reason, he turned his eyes away from Slocum's and kept his mouth shut.

Boyd managed to look embarrassed for his father, grateful to his friend, resentful of the implied slur to his family, and sad that Slocum was leaving, all at the same time.

Quite a trick, Slocum thought. He took the kid by the shoulder and gave him a fond shake. "You take care, kid." He swung lightly onto the sagging, bony back of the gift horse—Slocum reminded himself to never, ever look the damn thing in the mouth—and was satisfied to find that it did not throw itself into a fit of bucking once he was aboard.

Warren Calder glared up at him. "I think you should know, Slocum, I have my doubts about you."

Slocum grinned down at him. "That's only fair, Warren. I got a passel of 'em about you, too. Ain't it nice that we'll be out of each other's hair permanent now."

"We'd better be," Calder said darkly.

Slocum had been about to kick the pony into motion, but now he stopped. "What is that supposed to mean, mister?"

"Just what I said. When you leave Calder Hall it had better be out of this whole part of the country. I still haven't decided about what my crew suspects, and—"

"You better stop right there, mister, or I'm liable to do that boy of yours a disservice." The long, practiced fingers of John Slocum's right hand were unconsciously flexing, and he was poised to draw the old Navy. Warren Calder was within an eyeblink of dying, although he didn't seem to know it.

"Dammit, Pa, leave him be," Boyd cried. "John's right. He's done nothing to hurt us. He wouldn't neither. So don't you go to thinking that somebody's always spying on you. Now leave him be before you push him too far, Pa.''

Calder did not like it, but at last he took a look at the scarred wooden butt of the Navy and at Slocum's hand hovering near it. Calder had seen the awesome speed of Slocum's draw once, and no man who had ever seen it could want to face it. He clamped his jaw shut and stepped back, but the look on his face was a killing look.

Slocum was damn well glad to be taking his leave of this place. He had come to genuinely like Boyd Calder, and he didn't want to leave the boy fatherless when he rode away.

"Good luck to you, rooster," he said. He touched the brim of his hat and heeled the pony in the ribs.

And whether Warren Calder liked it or not, the road he took away from Calder Hall was the road that led to The Oaks.

37

"Would you care to go for a canter this afternoon, John?" Libby Ashford asked over the rim of her wine glass after lunch the next day.

Slocum had to laugh. "Darling Libby, you are gracious and you are beautiful and you are a tip-top bedroom companion. But you don't know the first thing about horseflesh if you think I would get on that wolf-bait horse of mine for the pleasure of it."

"I am not quite the total fool, John, and I do happen to own more than one horse."

"Did you have something particular in mind?"

"Actually, I did. There is a hammock not too awfully far from here where the afternoon light is really quite delightful. I have often wondered what it would be like to have a strong man make love to me there."

"In that case, lady . . ."

She smiled. In a louder voice she called, "Lem!"

The parlor door opened almost immediately. "Yes'm?"

"We shall need two horses saddled. We shall be riding to the glade below the old Fenster homestead."

"Yes'm." The black giant bobbed his head and ducked out of sight. Slocum was continually finding himself forgetting that the huge, machete-wielding former slave was always within the sound of Libby's voice. Which was not entirely bad. Remembering that Lem was around was far worse than being able to forget him. It was just as well that Libby Ashford did not have Rose Calder's sexual tastes, Slocum realized.

They finished their wine without hurry, and when they walked outside there was a pair of fine horses saddled and waiting for them.

The glade Libby had in mind was an hour's ride away, but in Libby's company for the first time Slocum was able to forget the heat and the constant swarms of insects that were always present here.

"What do you think?" she asked when they had arrived in the shadowed and—Slocum almost hated to admit it—lovely hammock.

There was a small grassy knoll in the center of the cypress hammock, surrounded by lacy ferns and festooned with drooping vines and wild orchids.

Most of the flowers Slocum did not even recognize as being flowers until Libby pointed out to him the tiny, almost invisible blooms on their spidery stalks.

"They are so delicate," she said.

"So are you." He touched her cheek and gently drew her face to him.

He tasted her lips, slowly at first and then more insistently as the desire built within him. He could feel her responding to his passion, pressing herself against him and manipulating the buttons of his shirt.

Slocum looked around. He could see no one, but he would not want to expose this elegant creature to public ridicule. And being caught in the midst of a sunlit romp would hardly enhance her reputation.

"Are you sure?"

"Very."

"What if someone came?"

"No one will."

He nodded, accepting her judgment. He stepped back from her and quickly stripped. He was already painfully erect, although they had spent much of the previous night enjoying each other's bodies.

Libby waited until she had his full attention before she removed her clothing. She did not try to make a game of it, but she seemed to enjoy his appreciation for the beauty she unveiled, and she undressed with her eyes on Slocum and a smile on her lips. When she was done, she posed for him, slim and beautifully nude in the dappled sun and shade of the hidden glade. The sight of her would have delighted a painter as she stood amid the ferns, Slocum thought. She stood with her chin high and a glow of anticipation in her cheeks.

"I approve," he said finally.

She held her arms out to him, and he entered the circle she created there for him.

He pressed her to the ground and lay beside her, the earth softened by moss and fallen ferns.

They lay together for some time, tasting of each other's lips and reversing to nip and nibble in a long, slow sixty-nine. Slocum ran his hands along the length of her legs and torso, lingering at her breasts and toying with her nipples while she gently sucked and pulled at the head and the shaft of his penis.

"Lovely," she whispered at one point.

"As good as your fantasies?"

"Mmm. Nicer, perhaps. This is real. Reality is always better than make-believe."

"Sh." He smiled. "Go back to what you were just doing, if you wouldn't mind."

"Mind? It would be my pleasure." Slowly she ran her tongue down the length of his shaft and lapped softly at his balls. She opened her lips wide apart and drew first one testicle and then the other into her mouth, warming them and delighting Slocum with the delicate sensations that ran through his groin and up his spine.

He caressed her cheek and temple and pulled her away, bringing her up beside him so that he could kiss her and taste the sweet honey of her breath.

He raised himself over her and felt her spread herself wide to his entry.

The long, slow glide into the wet depths of her was warm and welcome after their foreplay.

"Raise up," she whispered. "Just a little."

He did as she asked, and Libby drew her thighs together so that Slocum lay straddling her but still socketed deep inside the heat of her willing body.

"Damn!"

She laughed. "Do you like it?"

"You feel as tight as a virgin."

"Yes, I thought you might like to have a virgin for a change. You must get tired of the same old hole."

"What a way for a lady to talk," he chided.

Libby laughed again. "This is hardly a ladylike position, dear. Besides, with you I am a woman, not a lady."

"With me, Miss Ashford, what you are is marvelous." He began to stroke in and out of that marvelous and now remarkably tight woman-flesh.

Libby's hips found his rhythm and joined him, lifting to meet him and falling away with each withdrawal. The tempo of their mating held, as regular as the swing of a pendulum, but the pleasure mounted with every stroke, filling Slocum's balls and belly until there was room for no more.

Almost slowly then, almost timing itself to the rhythm of their bodies, the cum flowed up Slocum's shaft and out into the dark, wet cavity of Libby Ashford's womb.

He felt it come, felt the slow, insistent flow, felt the warm flood rather than an explosion this time, and he found it strange. Delightful and different but very, very strange.

When he was done and could hide the climax from her no more, his shoulders quivered in a violent shudder, and he allowed himself to relax on top of her body, remaining inside her and enjoying the warmth of her.

"Was that all right?" she asked long minutes later when he felt up to raising his head and looking at her.

"Incredible," he said. "I've never felt anything like that before. Never. It was . . . gentle. Very quiet. I liked it. I couldn't believe how complete it was. But I'm sorry you didn't make it too. I wanted you to."

She smiled. "But I did."

"You're kidding."

She shook her head. "Really. Very quietly. Very slowly. Very completely. And I think I shall never enter this glade again without remembering it."

"I never even noticed."

"I did," she said with a soft laugh. "Believe me, I did."

They lay together for some time longer until Slocum noticed that the sun was close to setting. He pulled her to her feet and they dressed and began the ride back to The Oaks without speaking. The afternoon was already complete. Nothing more needed to be added. They rode with the horses side by side, holding hands.

38

They were within a couple miles of The Oaks. Slocum remembered a clump of wild blueberry bushes there, the lightning scar on an oak trunk there. He glanced toward the western sky and doubted that they would be there before it was fully dark, because the dusk was already heavy. Not that it made a great deal of difference. They had already returned to the public road, and there would be no obstacles now that a half-blind horse could not avoid.

The afternoon had been more than enjoyable. And this entire thing with Libby Ashford was giving John Slocum a look—indeed an invitation, if he would welcome one—into a way of life that was far different from the rough-and-tumble he had come to accept as normal.

He was thinking about that. Idly wondering if it might be possible for a lean and hungry hunting leopard to change its spots.

His reverie was interrupted by the sound of footsteps and the crackle of branches from the road ahead.

Instinctively Slocum jumped his horse in front of Libby's, and the Navy Colt appeared in his hand with a magician's speed.

A gray-haired Negro came into sight, panting and staggering from the exertions of his run. He was lumbering forward in that untidy gait caused by extreme fatigue, but he was still making good time and seemed intent on speed.

"Jonah?" Slocum heard Libby behind him. "What is it, Jonah?"

The black ran past them, though, and crashed into the

undergrowth beside their horses, making Slocum's mount rear and fidget.

Slocum looked in the direction Jonah had run. There was brush in between, but he thought he could see Jonah, almost swallowed in the shadows of near-night, and another form as well.

"What the hell?"

"Don't ask me," Libby said.

"Is that one of your people?"

"Yes."

"But . . ."

They got their answer a moment later. Jonah came back to the road, more slowly this time and still heaving and gasping. There was another and far larger figure with him, and Slocum recognized the second man as the giant Lem.

Slocum looked incredulously toward Libby. "Has he been with us the whole damn time?"

"Of course."

"And you knew he was there watching?"

"Don't be silly. Lem would not watch. He only listens."

"Jesus." Slocum shook his head.

The worst part of it was not the private activities he and Libby had been engaged in that afternoon. The worst part was that Lem had been able to ghost along with them—and afoot at that—so silently that Slocum had never suspected the man was there. That was frightening. Nobody should be that good.

Still, it was immaterial now. And Lem *was* that good.

"Mist'ess."

"Yes, Lem?"

"Jonah heah, he jus' got word from Calder Hall. One o' the people there done run ovuh to tell us. Mista Calder heerd somethin' about Mista Slocum bein' heah an' bein' yo spy, an' that bunch from Calder Hall is comin' to shoot up Th' Oaks, mis'tess, an' burn it down, too."

"Shee-it," Slocum said. He let out a low whistle.

"They's on de way already, mist'ess," Lem said.

Libby's eyes were wide. "I don't know—"

"How many?" Slocum demanded, ignoring the woman for the moment. If they were already on their way there was no time to waste on questions like why. The first order of business was to stop them. Then Slocum could take the time to wonder.

Lem looked at him but refused to answer until he had gotten a nod from his mistress. "All o' them," he said.

Again Slocum whistled. One man against probably sixteen or seventeen. Tall odds for even the most desperate gambler.

It would not have occurred to Slocum, though, that this might not be his fight. He could have turned and ridden away and no one would ever know about it on the other side of the Mississippi. Except himself. And that would have been one too many. The only one that counted.

"I want you to stay away from The Oaks for a little while, Libby. I want you to stay out of my way."

"But, John . . ."

"Hush, woman. I've told you some of the things I've done. Well, this is what I do. Killing men is what I'm good for. Maybe the only thing I'm good for. So take advantage of it while you can. It's the only way you'll save The Oaks tonight, and I care for you too much to let them burn it."

She started to speak, but he cut her short. "I won't have time to listen to any arguments. Just promise me you'll stay out of the way. I don't want to have to worry about who I'm shooting at."

She nodded. "Lem, I want you to go with Mr. Slocum."

"But, mist'ess . . ."

"Don't argue with me, Lemuel. If you want to protect me, help Mr. Slocum protect The Oaks. Jonah can stay here with me. We will stay clear of the road, where no one can find us. Go on now."

Slocum was willing to give Lem some orders, but when he looked for the giant, the huge man had disappeared. It was fully dark now, and there was no trace of him anywhere on the road. Slocum had neither seen nor heard him go. One moment Lem was there talking to them and the next he had gone. He left no more trace of his passage than a puff of cigar smoke swept away by the wind.

Slocum waited until Libby and Jonah were clear of the road, then he checked the loads in the Navy and put his horse into a jog. He didn't have time to worry about what was behind him.

39

Given a choice, Slocum would have wanted some time to search the house. Libby's father must surely have left some guns behind, and a rifle or—far better—a shotgun would have been more than welcome.

A single revolver loaded with five shots—the sixth chamber of a cap-and-ball revolver is useless because the recoil of the first shot will throw off the percussion cap from the unprotected sixth nipple—is damn small defense against a crowd of armed and angry raiders.

There was not time enough for that, though, nor even for Slocum to try to set up an effective ambush. Ned Buntline stories about stand-up gunfights be damned; in a situation like this Slocum would gladly have reduced the odds by dropping as many of the Calder crackers as he could from hiding. John Slocum liked to win and to survive, and the hell with fancy theories about form and honor. In a real-life gunfight it was the man who walked away who was the victor, regardless of how he accomplished it.

There was just no time, though.

Slocum brought the borrowed horse into the yard of The Oaks at a gallop in time to see the first of Warren Calder's cowboys pounding down the road from the opposite direction with their pistols drawn and the well-remembered, high-pitched rebel yell on their lips.

The sound of that fondly recalled rallying cry stabbed deep into Slocum. Always before he had ridden *with* the men who used it. And now they were his enemy.

No matter what Warren Calder was or had been, he realized, some of these damnable Florida cowboys had also worn the gray of the Confederacy.

Still, on this night they were Slocum's enemy if he intended to save The Oaks for Elizabeth Ashford.

He jumped the horse into the teeth of their charge, wishing for that instant that there was the cold steel of a saber in his right fist, and a loud, ululating rebel yell was wrenched from Slocum's own throat before he even realized it.

At that one fleeting instant he might well have been wearing a floppy-brimmed Kossuth hat and have had a squadron of his good Arkansawyers at his side.

Lances of yellow flame spat like lightning bolts in the darkness as the nearest of the Calder men began to fire their revolvers, but Slocum was among them before they could begin to adjust to the fact that their charge was being countered or by whom or how many.

The night was Slocum's cloak and ally now, and the confusion he could strike into them was on his side.

Libby's tall, powerful horse was no stable dandy. It charged into the melee with a will and knocked the first of the crackers' cow ponies to its knees like a jousting knight battering his enemy to the ground.

Noise and confusion swirled all around Slocum in the darkness. Men were shouting and firing into the night without apparent purpose.

Slocum saw the pale moon of a man's face in the gloom and lashed out with the barrel of his Colt, striking the man on the side of the head and sending him reeling from the saddle.

Hoofbeats flashed nearby, and another yellow spear of exploding gunfire illuminated the scene.

A cowboy threw a shot that whistled near Slocum's ear, and John responded with a snap shot of his own that took the man in the throat and snapped his head back. Slocum did not see him fall, because by then the tall thoroughbred had dashed beyond and was charging the main body of the shouting crackers.

Some were carrying torches, obviously intent on firing the house, and Slocum hauled his horse's head around toward them.

Most of the Calder men were milling on their excited mounts, aware by now that an enemy was in their midst in the night, but one of the torchmen cut away from the others and spurred his pony into a dash toward the house.

There were too many in between for Slocum to be sure of a hasty shot from the Navy. He stabbed the big horse with his heels and tried to make his way forward to cut off the man with the torch.

Dimly, Slocum could see a shadow rise up from the ground between the Calder torchman and the big, columned house.

Torchlight flickered on a whistling steel blade, and the torch carrier toppled from his horse with dark blood spewing in a broad sheet from the place where his head and half of his right shoulder had been. The torch fell harmlessly to the ground.

Lem. Slocum had forgotten about Libby Ashford's protector, but the big black was here and was protecting his mistress.

A gunshot sounded at Slocum's back, and a lead ball slashed through Slocum's shirt, burning his ribs.

Slocum turned in the saddle and sent a .36-caliber ball of his own into the cowboy's chest. He had only three shots remaining.

Slocum charged the horse into a knot of horses and men that he could see by the torchlight. Both men and ponies reeled and stumbled as the big thoroughbred smashed its way through them and Slocum cut left and right with the barrel of the Navy.

The Calder men were confused and frightened now. They had expected to be able to overwhelm the lone man they expected to find opposing them.

Instead, the night was alive with danger. The tall, lean, powerful man on the big thoroughbred knocked them sprawling whenever they stood for his attack.

And any shadow might be transformed into a slashing machete that would cut through an arm as easily as a butcher knife through butter.

The least forceful among the Calder hands began to slip away in the night and turn their ponies toward the safety and the comforts of the bunkhouse, rationalizing that they could always claim to have become separated from the others in the dark.

Another torchman raced for the house only to find John Slocum and the tall, sweat-lathered thoroughbred before him. With the torch in one hand and a Remington revolver in the other, the cracker charged ahead. He raised his pistol and sighted on Slocum's belly.

The grinning westerner watched him come, seemed willing to wait for him to close, seemed in no hurry to raise and aim his pistol, and the cowboy felt a rush of fierce joy at the thought that he would get off the first shot.

But Slocum's hand tilted the slender barrel of the Navy without raising it to take a marksman's slow aim, and the third ball spat out to rip away the right side of the cracker's jaw and send him spilling out of the saddle with his torch forgotten and his life's blood flowing into the Florida sand.

Slocum saw another cowboy fall as his horse bucked him past a shadow that might have been a bush but instead was the giant Lem.

The hands that had held the pony's reins fell on one side of the horse while the Calder rider fell on the opposite side with a scream of rawest agony.

Two of the crackers saw their comrade go down. They leveled their pistols at the moving shadow and charged him on their quick-footed horses.

Slocum shot one from the saddle as they charged. The other raced past the shadow and fell with his belly sliced open and a steaming rope of intestines tangling his own feet and sliming his useless legs with fresh blood.

"Goddamnit, I don't believe this."

The voice cut through the shouting and the shooting, and the crackers hauled their panicky horses to a stop.

The voice was easily recognizable. Warren Calder

had finally consented to arrive on the scene, Slocum thought with contempt. Any man who was worth a shit would have been leading his own charge. Warren Calder had not been.

"What the fuck has happened here?" Calder demanded in a loud voice. There were rather few of his hands who were still mounted and able to guide their horses to him as a rallying point. Some of the missing were dead or injured, others had run away. In the darkness Slocum could not be sure, but he thought there were no more than four or five who were still in a condition to fight.

Slocum calmed the prancing, fidgeting thoroughbred and walked it with soft footfalls toward Calder and his men. He wondered about Boyd. He was sure the kid would have been in the thick of that first charge. He still liked the boy enough to hope that he was not one of those who had died.

"What . . . ?" Calder seemed unable to go on.

The cowboy who was beside him shrugged and turned his head away. "There was . . . Jesus, boss, we don't know how many. They was waiting for us. They was *every*where. Ridin', cuttin', Christ, we're just lucky there's any of us left alive."

Slocum grinned savagely into the gloom that surrounded him. Two men. And only one of those armed with a gun. Their determination and the confusion in the minds of the attackers had been enough to convince the crackers that they were fighting a troop if not a whole army of Ashford defenders.

The tall thoroughbred shouldered its way into the group, and Slocum sat looking Warren Calder in the eyes from a distance of no more than a yard.

"You played hell, Warren. These boys fought for you. Too many of them died for you. I don't even know why. Do they?"

"I . . ." Calder groped for words. He seemed to be seeing a ghost. Or was wishing that Slocum was a ghost. "Boyd admitted that he told you what I planned to do here, hoping you'd help. I . . . had to keep you from telling the squatters.''

"You poor, sad, stupid sonuvabitch," Slocum said. "The fact is, I don't much give a shit what happens down in this part of the country. An' I like your boy, Warren. You're a shit and a sonuvabitch, but you've got a good kid there. I wasn't figuring to say a word about it. And these cowboys of yours? Is that what you told them? That they were going to fight and maybe die because you're greedy and wanted to be richer than you are?" He shook his head. "Somehow, Warren, I don't think that is quite what you told them."

"What he told us," one of the men said in a low voice of tight-reined anger, "was that you was getting up an army o' squatters to come burn us out. We was going to get our licks in first. Shit, man, I'm comin' to think we was wrong about you." He jerked his head toward his employer—or, Slocum thought, more likely his *former* employer—and even a man as uncaring about the opinion of others as John Slocum was would not have enjoyed being the recipient of that kind of hatred as was in the cowboy's eyes. "I think we been wrong about *him,* too."

The Calder men began to rein their ponies away, and within seconds only Slocum and Warren Calder remained.

"You know, Warren," Slocum said, "I think it might not be a bad idea for you to think about moving to another part of the country. I don't think things are gonna be real pleasant for you around here in the future."

Calder swallowed. He seemed dazed. He nodded.

"Another thing," Slocum said. "You haven't asked about him. And I ain't seen him that I know of. But if I was you, I'd start looking for that boy of yours. He's layin' on the ground somewhere around here. The only question is whether he's alive or dead."

Calder swallowed hard again. Slocum was not sure whether in his trance he had heard and understood or not. Boyd Calder, live or dead, deserved better than this for a father.

Warren Calder had a revolver at his belt. Slocum did not have enough respect for the man to care. He turned the still fidgeting thoroughbred, turned his back on Warren Calder, and rode back toward the lights showing in The Oaks. There was no sign of Lem, but Slocum was not worried about the giant. By now, he figured, Lem would be halfway back to where Libby was waiting. Lem would be going about the business of protecting his mistress, and that was as it should be.

Slocum left the horse and took a seat on the edge of the broad, columned porch at the front of the house. It seemed a good place to wait.

40

Slocum put the last of his things into the saddlebags Libby had given him and buckled the bags closed. He was well-outfitted now, better than he had been to begin with, actually, with things that had belonged to Libby's war hero father.

"That seems to be it," he said.

"I wish you would change your mind," she said softly.

He did not look at her. When he did, the temptation to stay was so strong that it worried him. Libby Ashford was a pinnacle high above the common level of womankind, and in a way John Slocum was more comfortable with Rose Calder's strange hungers than with Libby Ashford's subtle, quicksand hold on him.

"Don't forget what I told you to do. Talk to the federal officers wherever the hell they are around here. They'll tell you how to go about it."

"I won't forget."

Warren Calder's plan to finally destroy the "squatters," as he insisted they should be called, had been garnered from his son's fascination with the west.

The Homestead Acts had been passed to allow settlers to gain title to the new lands being opened in the western territories, but as federal law, the acts covered any unowned lands in the nation. It had been Calder's plan to have his family and his employees file claims on the open range used by his neighbors so he could force them from their homes and create for himself a cattle empire in the swampy grasslands of central Florida.

Now, his power broken, the families he would have

driven away could file their own claims. And, Libby had realized, they would have an advantage of numbers that Warren Calder would never have had available to him. The hundreds of former slaves still living in the area and now on friendly terms with their former owners could file claims as well, and sell or lease the grazing rights to the stock raisers in the area.

Already Calder servants were showing up at the back door of The Oaks looking for work and for food.

The Calders, they said, were busy packing.

Boyd, Slocum had been glad to hear, was too badly injured to help with the packing. But the kid would live.

That was something.

Slocum sighed. He turned and took Libby in his arms.

"One last time, John?"

"We did it one last time all last night," he reminded her.

"I'm not so sore that I couldn't stand just one more," she said with a smile. "Not quite."

Slocum laughed. "We'll both be walking bowlegged for a month. And I have a lot of miles to cover."

The big thoroughbred, another gift she had pressed on him but one he had offered no protest to, was already saddled and waiting out front, he knew.

"I don't know that I could leave you after one more taste of you," he admitted.

"That's the best reason I've ever heard for taking off my clothes."

He shook his head. "I have to go."

"If you ever find the time, John, or the inclination, I shall be here. Anytime you want, any way you want me. If you need to rest or heal, you will always have a home here. If you ever send word that you want me, I shall join you. Anytime. Anyplace you wish. I promise you that."

He held her so tightly that he must have hurt her, but she made no protest.

Quickly, before he might be tempted beyond his ability to resist, he let go of her and turned to walk swiftly away.

He did not look at her again.

JAKE LOGAN

_____ 21217	SLOCUM AND THE MAD MAJOR	$1.95
_____ 21,120	SLOCUM AND THE WIDOW KATE	$1.95
_____ 16880	SLOCUM'S BLOOD	$1.95
_____ 16823	SLOCUM'S CODE	$1.95
_____ 21071	SLOCUM'S DEBT	$1.95
_____ 16867	SLOCUM'S FIRE	$1.95
_____ 16856	SLOCUM'S FLAG	$1.95
_____ 21015	SLOCUM'S GAMBLE	$1.95
_____ 21090	SLOCUM'S GOLD	$1.95
_____ 16841	SLOCUM'S GRAVE	$1.95
_____ 21023	SLOCUM'S HELL	$1.95
_____ 16764	SLOCUM'S RAGE	$1.95
_____ 16863	SLOCUM'S RAID	$1.95
_____ 21087	SLOCUM'S REVENGE	$1.95
_____ 16927	SLOCUM'S RUN	$1.95
_____ 16936	SLOCUM'S SLAUGHTER	$1.95
_____ 21163	SLOCUM'S WOMAN	$1.95
_____ 16864	WHITE HELL	$1.95

582-23